R.T.J. Hockin grew up in Mousehole, Cornwall. He is a keen surfer and works for Devon & Cornwall Police. He lives with his family near St. Ives Bay.

Have You
Seen Joe?

R. T. J. Hockin

Have You Seen Joe?

Nightingale Books

NIGHTINGALE PAPERBACK

A CIP catalogue record for this title is
available from the British Library.

ISBN 978 1 91202 169 7

Nightingale Books is an imprint of
Pegasus Elliot MacKenzie Publishers Ltd.
www.pegasuspublishers.com

First Published in 2018

Nightingale Books
Sheraton House Castle Park
Cambridge England

Printed & Bound in Great Britain

Dedication

To Isaac, Lucia & Gabe, in memory of Teddy
Edward, Nam Nam and Minky.

Acknowledgements

I would like to thank the following;

The staff at the Cornwall Family History Society in Truro who kindly assisted me with my family tree research which underpins this story,

My brother-in-law Joe Mason for producing such fabulous illustrations which have served to really bring this adventure story to life.

The team at Pegasus Elliot Mackenzie Publishers for their excellent guidance throughout this journey.

And to my wife, Danielle, for her unwavering support and encouragement in all that I do.

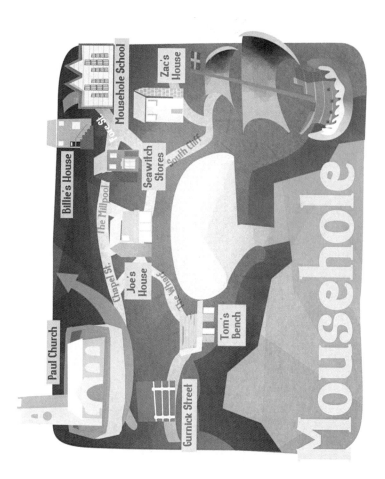

Paul Church

Billie's House

Mousehole School

Jones St.

Zac's House

Seawitch Stores

South Cliff

The Millpool

Chapel St.

Joe's House

The Wharf

Tom's Bench

Gurnick Street

Mousehole

Chapter 1 – Grounded

'Have you seen Joe? Mrs Berryman, have *you* seen Joe?'

The old lady stopped, put her shopping bags down on the roadside then looked up at John Pentreath who was marching towards her with a frazzled expression on his face.

'What's up, John, lost the boy again? You need a leash for him!' she joked, but John Pentreath was not amused.

'This is the third time this week that he's been late home. I haven't got time to be running around after him like this. He'll have to be grounded this time!'

'Calm down, John, you were just the same when you were his age, always off daydreaming somewhere, used to drive your dad to his wits' end. I remember. Now have you checked down the South Quay? I have seen Joe down there a lot of late, talking with Tom.'

'Hmm, thanks,' John replied and set off 'marching' once again.

Mousehole is a beautiful fishing village situated at the very far end of Cornwall and its harbour is the beating heart of village life. On stormy days people like to come and watch the waves crashing over the harbour walls and pounding on the cars that park there, usually left by some poor unsuspecting person who will return to find their car covered in seaweed and not wanting to start again. One year a car was actually washed off the quayside and into the harbour. Now that would spoil your holiday somewhat!

And then there are beautiful sunny days, like today, when the sky is blue, the tide in full and children laughing and screaming as they enjoy playing on their kayaks. The younger children pretend that they are pirates, whilst the older ones dive off the quayside doing their best to show off to the holidaymakers who gather to be amused.

John Pentreath had already scanned the children playing in the water to see if Joe was amongst them, but he knew he wouldn't be and so he headed off towards the South Quay to find old Tom.

Tom Tregenza had lived in Mousehole all of his very long life. The village is blessed with quite a number of locals now well over 80 years old, who have never wanted to leave the village and so have grown up and grown old together. Tom is oldest of all, fast approaching his 100th birthday on the 23rd of July. John knew where to find Tom. As ever Tom was sat on the benches gazing out to sea, whilst his faithful collie dog, Patch, lay peacefully asleep at his feet.

They say that when Tom was a young boy, he was full of mischief and talked nineteen to the dozen.

'You can always hear Tom before you see him.' That's what the grown-ups used to say. But then on his thirteenth birthday Tom fell silent, barely a word has passed his lips from that day to this.

'Tom!' John called out as he approached the old man.

'Tom, have you seen Joe?'

Without taking his eyes off the sea's horizon, Tom simply replied,

'Aye – Merlin Rock.'

He raised his right hand and pointed along the coastline. Patch roused from his slumber, looked up at John Pentreath and barked in agreement.

John looked in the direction that the old man was pointing and sure enough out towards Merlin Rock he could see his son, standing there as if frozen, staring at the horizon.

With a mixture of relief and anger, John let out a mighty roar:

'Joseph Pentreath, get here now!'

****

Joe was miles away. Not literally of course because he was on Mousehole beach about to get told off by his dad. Rather his mind was miles away. Whilst gazing at the horizon, Joe was dreaming about ships. Not big container ships or the countless trawlers he would see each day, but big old-fashioned galleons with massive sails and cannons firing from all sides. Joe loved to daydream. He had a vivid imagination and would often fantasise about being an explorer, sailing off to new lands and finding treasure and then doing battle with terrifying pirates. As his mind wondered he stared out to sea, and the longer he stared out to sea, the more real his dream seemed to become. First of all he could make out a dot on the horizon which seemed to be getting bigger. Then a second dot, followed by a third and then finally a fourth. At first Joe thought that they must be a trawler fleet returning home to Newlyn after a successful few weeks away, but the dots weren't aiming for Newlyn, they were coming straight towards Mousehole, in fact straight towards Joe.

As the dots got bigger, Joe could start to make out their shapes. His eyes strained, something looked different about these ships. He concentrated all of his focus on the four ships and, just as he thought he could make out that these actually *were* galleons, his dad's booming voice snapped his concentration.

'Joseph, here NOW!'

Joe turned sharply and looked back towards the village. He could see his dad stood next to old Tom at the benches on the harbour wall at the other end of the beach. His heart sank.

Oh no, he thought to himself. *I'm late home again.*

As he started to scramble back over the rocks towards his dad he cast a look over his right shoulder towards the approaching ships, but there were no approaching ships, not one. The sea was clear with the exception of four men on kayaks making in for the harbour. Joe stopped. He couldn't believe his eyes. Where had those huge ships gone?

'NOW, JOE!' his dad bellowed.

Confused, Joe set off once more. When you have scrambled over rocks since you were a baby, you are very adept at picking the best course. Your eyes move quickly assessing each rock, your brain decides instantly if any rock is too slippery or likely to move under your weight and your body simply trusts and automatically follows, meaning that children like Joe can cross a rocky beach in moments. As he got closer to his dad he could see just how annoyed his father was and he knew he was in real trouble, this time.

'Home, dinner and bed for you, young man,' His dad fired out once Joe was stood next to him.

'But, Dad,' Joe tried to reason.

'No buts. And you are grounded for a whole week!'

Joe couldn't speak. His heart felt heavy, his throat felt choked and he knew he was going to cry. He didn't want his dad or old Tom to see him cry so he stared down at Patch who was stretched out in the sun, asleep once more.

Suddenly old Tom stood up, sprightly, back straight as a rod and he looked John Pentreath straight in the eyes.

'Lad can't help it John, it's calling him, ain't that right, Joe?'

Joe looked up at the old man and for the first time ever saw the old man wink at him and a sly smile crossed his lips.

Chapter 2 – Bored

Joe hated being grounded, especially on sunny days. He sat at his bedroom window and stared out at the hustle and bustle of people going about their Saturday morning business. Joe's bedroom is at the front of their house directly above his mum and dad's restaurant which is on the seafront overlooking the harbour.

As he sat in silence he could hear his mum crashing and banging around downstairs as she got the restaurant ready for another busy day. His dad, who had not spoken to him since he had given him an almighty telling-off the previous evening, had gone over to the fish auction at Newlyn market.

Bored. So bored. Joe looked to the sea. Some of his friends were down in the harbour, setting up an impromptu football match. Joe got on well with all the lads in his year at school, but Billie and Zack were his favourites. If Joe was down in the harbour now, Zack would be one of the captains and he would always pick Joe and Billie first.

If they weren't playing in the harbour then the three of them enjoyed going on adventures around the lanes on their bikes. Sometimes they would go as far as the woods in Lamorna and spend the day setting up rope swings. They really enjoyed this because the older boys weren't around to push in and take over. That had happened the last time they had set up a swing on one of the few trees in Mousehole. A group of lads from the year above found them and demanded that the swing was now theirs and that Joe, Billie and Zack should get lost or else they would tie the three of them to a tree and leave them there for the rats to feast on!

Zack had been very upset by this as it was his dad's rope that they had used to make the swing and Zack had been the one brave enough to climb to the highest branch and tie the knot. Zack's upset had turned to anger and his face suddenly became bright red. Joe could remember seeing tears in Zack's eyes. As Joe and Billie backed away from the bigger boys, Zack stood his ground. The bigger boys had laughed at Zack.

'Oooo tough man!' Jim Williams, the leader of the Year Seven boys mocked and he shoved Zack so hard that Zack flew backwards into a patch of stinging nettles. The whole group of Year Sevens stood over him pointing and laughing. Billie, usually the quietest and calmest of the three friends and being as tall if not taller than the Year Seven boys, did not hesitate in taking action. He walked straight up to Jim Williams and punched him hard on the nose. Instantly his nose seemed to explode and blood streamed down his pristine white brand new Holister T-shirt.

Williams started to cry like a baby. Acting quickly whilst everyone was distracted, Joe pulled Zack out of the nettle patch and shouted 'Run!' to Billie who was squaring up to hit Williams again. The three boys ran for their lives as the ten Year Seven lads recovered from their shock and started to chase after them.

Joe smiled to himself at the thought. As much as he enjoyed their adventures, he also liked some time to himself, to be alone with his imagination. Not like this though, he sighed, trapped in his room. No, he liked to be outside whenever he could, letting his daydreams run wild. Sometimes he would make boats with things he found washed up on the beach. Some polystyrene for the hull and cabin and a lolly stick to hold it all together. He would throw it into the sea on a stormy day and see if it could survive the endless pounding from the crashing waves and make its way to the safety of deeper water. He would pretend that he was the captain on board. He enjoyed the feeling of excitement, his blood racing. Could he get his crew to safety? Joe could get so caught up in his daydreams that in his mind, for those few moments, the adventure was real and the boring things in life like school, homework, Year Seven bullies and tidying your room, simply did not exist.

Even now, cooped up in his room, Joe's mind started to wonder once more. His anger at his dad for grounding him had started to ease and his frustration at not being down in the harbour with Billie and Zack slipped to the back of his mind. Something old Tom had said yesterday started to play with his thoughts...

'Lad can't help it, John, it's calling him.'

What did he mean? What was calling him?

He gazed out of his window, over the people in the street, past his friends in the harbour and out onto the long blue twinkling sea that stretched to the horizon.

'The horizon!' Joe said out loud. The horizon had been calling him. He hadn't realised it, but now that he came to think about it, every day after school for the past week he had raced home, thrown his school clothes on his bedroom floor, pulled on the same pair of shorts and T-shirt and made his way to the beach which lay beyond the South Quay. And every day he ended up gazing out to sea. Joe strained his mind, trying to recall just what he had been daydreaming about whilst he had been looking out to sea, but nothing came.

He could remember the same process – sitting in school, staring at the clock, desperate for the bell to ring at half past three. Every time he checked the clock it always seemed to say a quarter to three. The impatience would well up inside him so strongly that he thought his body was going to overpower his mind. Some days he thought he could fight it no longer and that at any moment his body would leap up and run out of the classroom, yet somehow his mind would restrain it and he would sit glued to his seat.

Once the beautiful bell of freedom had sounded he was up, grabbing coat and bag, he was the first out of the door. Usually he would wonder home discussing adventure plans with

Billie and Zack, but every day for this last week he had run off alone leaving Billie and Zack confused and somewhat annoyed with him. Each day had been the same; make for Merlin Rock at the far end of the beach then sit there, mind wondering, eyes fixed on the horizon. He couldn't really recall any great detail as to what he had been thinking about, nor could he recall seeing anything of note, until yesterday when he saw the four dots approaching. He still couldn't quite understand that. He was sure he had seen four large old-style sailing ships but when he had looked again there were only four men on kayaks. The one thing he could recall however, was that each day when he made the return walk home, Tom was there, sat on his bench at the end of the South Quay, Patch sat dutifully at his feet, both gazing at the same spot on the horizon and each day all Tom would say as Joe walked past was:

'Nothing today, Joe. Maybe tomorrow.'

Joe's thoughts returned to the present. Gazing out over the North Quay did not seem as captivating as the view past the South Quay. He looked at his bedside clock. Still only half past ten. Dad had confiscated his mobile and his laptop so his room was starting to feel more like a prison cell. He was still allowed to mope around the rest of the house, so he thought he would go downstairs and get himself a drink.

One benefit of owning a restaurant, there was always plenty of food and drink around. As he opened the fridge door to select a nice cool can of coke, his mum's voice suddenly sounded behind him.

'Ah just the lad, give me a hand to set the tables for the lunch time rush, will you?'

'I was just about to have a drink,' Joe retorted in an *I'm in a bad mood* type of way.

'Well there's plenty of water in the tap or you can help me, then you can have the drink of coke and I'll even let you have a slice of cake, how about that?'

'Fine,' he said, meaning it wasn't really fine but what choice did he have. Actually he did like helping out in the restaurant. He was fascinated by all the different types of people who would come in for refreshment. The restaurant was well supported by the local people but Joe was always fascinated by the many thousands of holiday makers that chose Mousehole as their favourite holiday location. Joe liked to see the differing fashion styles and enjoyed listening in to the conversations. He liked to try and guess which country the travellers were from.

Joe decided that he would help by polishing the cutlery. He filled a jug with hot water and firstly put all the knives in. He liked the warm feeling between his fingers as he pulled the hot knives through the tea towel and he liked the instant reward of seeing the dull piece of cutlery suddenly gleam and shine in the restaurant lights. It was also a job that Joe had done many times before, so now at the grand old age of eleven he had mastered the skill which now came as second nature to him. This meant that he could allow his mind to wander and still do the job properly. Once again old Tom popped up in his thoughts. After a few moments of pondering Joe suddenly broke the silence in the room.

'Mum, why does old Tom spend every day by himself just staring out to sea? And why doesn't he say very much?'

'Well,' Joe's mum began, 'Your dad told me that your grandfather told him that Tom Tregenza was once a very happy young lad who liked nothing more than playing tricks on people and making up tall stories that used to keep all the younger children in the village entertained. But then, around the time of his thirteenth birthday, the younger children started to complain to their parents that Tom was telling them scary stories about the village being burnt

down and the children being killed. Hmm –
something else happened, but I can't remember.
You should ask Dad.'

Joe's mum hadn't grown up in Cornwall,
unlike his dad who had grown up in the very
house that they lived in as had his dad and his dad
before that. In fact they say that there have been
Pentreath's in Mousehole for over five hundred
years.

Joe's mum had come to Cornwall with her
parents for their summer holidays every year
ever since she was a little girl. One year her
family spent their holiday in Mousehole to
celebrate her eighteenth birthday. Joe's dad
always says that he saw her sat alone on the
harbour wall one sunny day, her long red hair
radiating like flames dancing in a fire. He says he
was instantly captivated by her beauty and they
would both embarrass Joe by telling him about
love at first sight. Needless to say, Joe's mum
never went back home after that particular
holiday and she had been in Mousehole ever
since.

'I don't know,' Joe said, 'I don't think Dad
wants to speak to me at the moment.'

'Of course he does!' his mum replied. 'He
loves you very much, Joe. He was just angry
because he was so worried. You were very late

last night. Now look he's just pulling up with the fresh fish, go and help him unload.'

Joe put down the last of the knives that he had been polishing and went out into the main street. He was glad to feel the sun on his face and he took in a deep breath of fresh, salty sea air.

'Thought you might want a hand, Dad,' he said to his father who was just opening the back doors of his van.

'Thanks, Joe, yes we need to get these into the fridge quickly.' As well as the trays of fish, Joe could see that his dad had been to the grocers as there were also crates of fresh fruit and veg. It took them a few trips to and from the van and, as they walked, Joe talked.

'Dad, Mum said you know a bit about old Tom.'

'A bit, there's not much to know as he rarely speaks to anyone, but I do know that if there is ever a problem in the village Tom will get involved and put things right. In fact if it wasn't for Tom you and I would not be here today.'

'Really. Why?' Joe asked.

'Well as you know Tom spends every day down on the benches on the South Quay, looking out to sea, with one of his dogs keeping him company. Actually he's had a dog for as long as I can remember, different ones of course. I guess he's owned quite a few over his long life. Anyway on this particular day Tom had old Barnaby with him. A red setter. That dog was getting on a bit, couldn't really see but had this amazing ability to sense trouble. Good job he could, as your grandfather had decided he was going to swim out to the island by himself. He was about fourteen at the time. Sure enough he swam out to the Island no problem, but halfway back he suddenly got cramp and started to drown. Well old Barnaby knew something was wrong and started to bark. Tom, who was about fifty at the time, looked up from repairing his fishing nets and saw your grandfather in trouble. Without hesitation he climbed up onto the harbour wall, dived in, swam to your grandfather and pulled him out just in time. So you see, you and I owe a lot to Tom Tregenza.'

'I didn't know that,' Joe said pausing to regain his train of thought after hearing this surprising news.

'Mum said something happened to Tom around his thirteenth birthday.'

Joe's dad stopped and set down the heavy crate that he had been carrying. He leant against the restaurant counter and looked Joe straight in the eyes.

'My father told me that Tom went missing on his thirteenth birthday. His parents thought it strange when he didn't wake them up early that morning full of excitement, like all children are on their birthdays. They went to his room and he was not there. They searched the house, the harbour and the streets but he was nowhere to be found. Apparently the entire village was out looking for him the whole day. Then late that evening he was seen by the groundsman up at Paul Church to come running out of the churchyard and racing as fast as he could down Paul Lane and back home. His face, they say, was white as a sheet and he had the look of terror in his eyes. He would not tell his parents what had happened to him and from that very day he was a changed boy. No more jokes. No more tricks and no more funny stories for the little 'uns.'

Joe stood transfixed by his father's story telling.

'Anyway,' his Dad suddenly said, snapping them both out of their trance. 'We are putting on a special meal for Tom's one hundredth birthday, here in the restaurant next week. We'll probably have to hire in more tables to put out in the street as everyone says they want to join in.'

Joe smiled then started to head back to his bedroom.

'Joe,' his dad called after him. 'Thanks for helping Mum and I this morning.' He paused. 'And I'm sorry I shouted at you.'

'I'm sorry that I scared you,' Joe said.

Joe and his Dad couldn't stay angry at each other for very long. They both smiled then gave each other a big hug.

'Go on, get out in the sun and have some fun,' his Dad whispered.

Chapter 3 – Free Again.

Joe set off to find Billie and Zack. He looked over into the harbour but by now the football match had finished and only the younger children were left making dams at the point the river meets the sea. He wondered along Cliff Road to the ice cream parlour.

'Hello, Mrs Treloar. Is Zack in?'

'Sorry, Joe, he and Billie have taken a packed lunch and gone off on their bikes for the day. They thought you were grounded. Got time off for good behaviour did you?'

Joe smiled and felt a little embarrassed, he could feel his cheeks starting to burn red. He quickly said goodbye and left the shop.

What to do now? he thought to himself. He started to aimlessly wander along the back roads of the village. First up Commercial Road then onto South View Terrace and before long he was ambling along 'The Millpool'. All the while his mind was wandering and his daydreaming had started once more. Without realising it, he had strolled right across to the south side of the village, down the steep steps at the end of

Gurnick Street and he was now standing on the rocks looking out to sea past the Merlin Rock.

It was an unsettled day today. The sky was a mixture of clear blue patches contrasted by large, almost dark purple clouds. It had started off as a day with a light breeze but as he stood at the water's edge, Joe could feel the wind stiffen with the occasional gust trying to blow him off his feet. When the wind starts to whip up like this the sea is transformed. One minute the sea could be tranquil, like a shimmering blue mirror, inviting you to come and play, the next minute it could look dark and menacing, unpredictable waves crashing over the rocks, each one clawing further up the beach trying to grab hold of something or someone and drag them back into the murky depths below. From a very young age, the children of Mousehole had learnt to respect the sea and they knew not to play with it when it was angry.

Suddenly Joe's daydreaming came to an abrupt end as a crash of thunder and a flash of lightning tore through the sky. Joe knew what was coming next. They started slowly. A splatter here, a splatter there, but their frequency picked up and soon the large heavy raindrops started to sting Joe's face. Standing out on the rocks by yourself in the middle of a thunderstorm is not a particularly good idea. So once again Joe found himself at the wrong end of South Quay beach needing to run across the rocks as fast as he could.

He set off, skipping gracefully from rock to rock. Fortunately, having crossed this beach so many times in his life, Joe knew the quickest and easiest route. At least he thought he did. The only problem is that when it is raining all of the rocks get wet and when they are wet it is very difficult to tell which ones are the dangerously slippy Blue Elgin and which ones are not. Another louder, very close clap of thunder distracted Joe, just as he was jumping across a rock pool. As he landed on the opposite side of the pool his left foot landed heavily on a Blue Elgin. No sooner had his foot touched the rock then it slipped out sideways. Joe twisted in mid-air. He yelled out as the pain, red hot, shot through his left ankle and up into his leg. He fell between the rocks and landed awkwardly on the shingle below, striking the side of his head as he ground to a halt. Everything went black.

****

'Hey! Are you all right? Can you hear me? Are you all right?'

Joe could hear the voice but everything was still dark. And the pain! His ankle was burning and how his head ached. Joe had never felt pain like it. He struggled to open his eyes as he found the light too bright. As he tried to focus, he pulled himself up into a seated position, leaning heavily against a smooth rock. The rock felt dry and very warm.

'Good, you are alive then,' the voice continued. 'Thought you had drowned and the sea had thrown you back, what with you lying there all soaked through.'

The headache started to ease and his eyes were now able to take in the surroundings.

Strange, he thought to himself, that storm must have passed over quickly. The sky was clear blue and the sea was once again like a shimmering mirror. The rocks were hot to touch but Joe's clothes were indeed soaking wet.

'What's the matter with you then? You haven't swallowed your tongue have you?'

For a moment Joe had forgotten that someone else was there. He looked up to see a young lad, maybe Joe's age perhaps a bit older. He couldn't seem to stand still and he kept hopping from rock to rock as he talked.

'So how long have you been lying around here?'

'I… I don't know. I fell over and…' Joe stammered.

'Interesting clothes you got on there, where you from then, not seen you in the village before?'

Joe stared blankly at this curious boy.

'Well are you from Nantewas? Or are you part of the travelling Gypsies? Anyway, what brings you to Porthenys?'

'I… I,' Joe began, rubbing the bump on his forehead which was throbbing. 'I'm from Mousehole, I've always lived here.'

The boy burst out laughing.

'Mousehole, where's that? What a silly name! There's no such place, you're messing with me. Good one, I like you. Come on, the others will be waiting for me, you can come too… what's your name?'

'Joe,' Joe mumbled in a dazed and very confused way.

'Well then, Joe from Mowzel, come on!'

The boy was active again, hopping nimbly over the rocks.

'Wait…'

'Henery!' the lad called back.

'Henery, where are we going?'

'Coosing,' came the reply. 'Hurry up!'

Joe started off over the rocks, gingerly at first as he regained his balance and his ankle got used to taking his weight. It didn't take long for him to shrug off his aches and pains and he was soon catching Henery up. As Joe's head began to clear he was able to take in some new sights and sounds. Firstly he noticed that the bay was busy with old-style sail-powered fishing boats. Secondly he noted that the harbour wall was covered in large black fishing nets, just like he had seen in the very old photographs from his History lessons. But most startling of all, Joe noticed that the houses along Gurnick Street were not the stone and brick buildings that he was used to. Rather the houses were much smaller wooden structures with thatched roofs – every one of them!

'Henery, wait. Wait!' Joe called out just as Henery had reached the end of the beach and disappeared behind the harbour wall and into the village itself.

Slightly panicking now, Joe sped up. He raced to the end of the beach and leapt up the small flight of steps that led to the harbour car park. Here came Joe's next shock. There were no cars in the car park. In fact there was no car park. Instead of the rows of cars that Joe was used to weaving in and out of there were market stalls and plenty of people busily going about their business.

As Joe tried to take on board the new sights and sounds he made sure that he kept his focus on Henery who was still ahead of him darting in and out of view. Joe did not want to lose him as Henery was his only hope of trying to figure out where he was and what had happened to him.

As Henery and Joe raced along the seafront, Joe recognised this area and when Henery turned the corner and ran up the steep incline, Joe knew exactly where he would end up. As Joe turned the corner he saw the instantly recognisable granite pillars of Keigwin House. There, standing directly in front, was Henery who was holding court with ten other children. These children, some as young as seven or eight, others in their early teens, were all hanging off every word that Henery was saying.

'Who's ready for coosing!' he bellowed.

'Yeah!' the group cheered, all becoming quite animated.

'First let me introduce a new player,' Henery said as he signalled to Joe to come and join him. Joe didn't like being the centre of attention so he felt very embarrassed as he stood in front of this eager group of onlookers.

'This is Joe from Mowzel,' Henery announced.

'Is that in another country, Joe? Did you swim here?' called out the smallest boy, much to the amusement of the rest of the group. Joe didn't answer. He couldn't answer. What would he say? One minute it was raining, he had fallen over and now it's sunny and everything here seemed familiar but also so different. Was this a dream? Perhaps he had fractured his skull when he'd fallen and he was actually lying in a coma in hospital.

Henery broke the awkward silence.

'Trevelyan, you lost the last coosing so you're the chief catcher this time,' he commanded, looking at one of the older lads. Trevelyan mumbled something and kicked a stone in disgust.

Henery turned to face Joe.

'Right Joe, Trevelyan here is going to try and catch one of us. Whoever he catches joins him as a catcher. They will then try and catch more of us to join their gang. The last one to be caught is the champion.'

'Henery is the best at coosing,' the outspoken little lad chipped in. 'He's always our champion!' He continued looking up adoringly at Henery.

'Thanks, Jack. Right everyone, let the coosing begin!'

Trevelyan, who was rather a rotund and heavily built lad, was the first person caught most of the time but today he spied his chance to make a quick catch. He could see that Joe had no idea as to what was going on, so as soon as Henery signalled the start, he lunged at Joe. Big strong hands were bearing down on Joe's collar. Joe froze, his eyes staring straight at Trevelyan's determined face. Just as those strong hands were about to seize their prey, Joe felt himself being lifted off his feet as he was propelled backwards.

'Oh no you don't!' called out Henery as he pulled Joe out of harm's way. Henery's years of experience came to Joe's assistance and Trevelyan missed out. As his lunge failed to make contact with Joe, Trevelyan was sent sprawling, face down into the dust. The younger children squealed with joy and took to their heels as quickly as they could.

'This way!' Henery shouted, as he sprinted off towards the winding alleyways in the heart of the village. Joe made sure that he kept close this time.

After turning just two corners Henery stopped running and merely ambled along. This took Joe by surprise and he bumped into Henery.

'Steady,' the older boy said calmly, 'look, there's no need to run anymore. It'll take Trev ages to make his first catch. Probably be one of the youngest he gets first, then the little 'uns will do all the work catching the others. Give it half an hour, then it'll get interesting.'

As they walked, Joe had his first real opportunity to take in his new surroundings. Some were familiar, like Keigwin House and its Square, the southern harbour wall and of course St Clement Island out to sea, covered in seagulls as always. But then so many things were different; there was no north harbour wall, there were many old-fashioned fishing boats to-ing and fro-ing the harbour and people, so many people. There were fishermen on the boats and all over the harbour wall, the streets dusty and bustling with women and children. Joe had never seen the village this hectic and noisy, even in the height of the summer holidays when the village welcomed tourists from all over the world. And the people themselves were different, all of them dressed in clothes the likes of which Joe had only ever seen in his history books.

With too much to take in Joe started to feel panicky once more and so he suddenly grabbed Henery by the arm and pulled him to a stop.

'Where am I Henery?' Joe almost pleaded.

'Porthenys of course,' Henery replied, looking quizzically at Joe.

Porthenys, Joe thought. He had learnt at school that Mousehole was once called Porthenys, but that was a very long time ago. That got Joe thinking.

'What year is this, Henery?'

'You must have really hit your head when you fell on the rocks. Knocked your brains out I reckon!' Henery had a playful glint in his eyes.

'Well?' Joe demanded, starting to feel both frustrated and scared.

'It's 1595 of course. Eighteenth of July 1595. Hey, it's my birthday in five days' time. Don't forget now, twenty-third of July. A very important day!' He laughed and punched Joe playfully on the shoulder.

Joe suddenly felt faint. The strength had gone from his legs. He felt weak and thought he was about to fall over.

'1595,' he mumbled, 'How can that be? It's impossible.' He could hear his blood rushing in his ears and his stomach had tightened into an anxious knot making him feel both light-headed and queasy.

'Look out! Seems Trevelyan is doing well today,' Henery called out as he took to his heels and sped off, once again niftily weaving between the street traders. Joe glanced behind him and saw Trevelyan lumbering around the corner. He had three of the younger children skipping around him awaiting their commands.

'There they are, get Joe!' Trevelyan's voice boomed and at that the little sprites were released and they homed in with Joe fixed in their sights.

Joe had played such chase and capture games many times at school and he was determined that he was not going to let Henery down by being caught by the little children. He pushed his worries to the back of his mind for a moment and set off. Joe had already lost sight of Henery so made his own decision to take a quick left turn and try and escape down a narrow alleyway. The lane ran between two rows of houses, which were built so closely together that no sunlight could break through. This made the alleyway both dark and damp. As Joe made his way through the darkness he could hear a commotion behind him.

'He ran down here, Trev.'

'Then we have him. That's a dead end!' Their laughter was ringing in Joe's ears as he realised what they had just said, but it was too late. Joe was running too fast and as he rounded a tight corner he tripped over something that lay on the ground in that dark and dank alley. He was sent head first into a solid wall. For the second time that day Joe felt a roaring pain in his head and in his ears.

And then silence…

Chapter 4 – Dazed and Confused.

'What's up? Having a snooze, Joe?' came a familiar voice. 'Best get yourself home before your father is out again shouting after you.'

As Joe slowly opened his eyes, he could see the round, kind face of old Mrs Berryman smiling down at him. He eased himself once more into a seated position, his ears still ringing slightly and head thumping.

'Funny place to take a lie-down, were you taking shelter from that thunderstorm?'

Joe looked about himself and was relieved to see familiar surroundings. He now found himself sat in the porchway at the rear of Mrs Berryman's cottage. Mrs Berryman's cottage was on Commercial Road and the alleyway that ran behind these houses is very narrow. Mrs Berryman lived right at the end.

Joe stood up.

'Oh. Oh yes, Mrs Berryman, the thunder was very loud and I thought I would get soaked by the rain,' he fibbed as he sidestepped the old lady.

'Hmmm. Whatever you say, dear,' she replied and gave him an all-knowing wink as she moved to open her front door. Joe, still slightly dazed and confused, said his goodbye and ambled off through the village, which he noted was back to its usual self; holidaymakers licking their ice creams, children playing on their kayaks in the harbour and cars driving cautiously through the narrow streets.

Although his head ached a little, Joe decided that he would not make straight for home. He needed some time alone with his thoughts and before long he was back down at the south quay wall, gazing out to sea.

What had just happened to him? Had he fallen asleep? Was that a dream? Maybe he had fallen and damaged his brain!

'All right then, lad?'

Joe was snapped out of his ponderings by Tom's question. He turned to see old Tom settling himself down on his usual bench.

'Oh yes fine thanks, Tom, just got a lot on my mind at the moment.'

'Thought you might have. Sometimes a problem shared, is a problem halved, if you think I may be able to help,' the old man enquired.

'Um… no. No, not at the moment. Thanks anyway,' Joe replied. He didn't feel that he could tell anyone what he thought had happened to him today. Grown-ups, Joe thought, always take everything so seriously. He didn't want this getting back to his parents. He worried that they would think he had damaged his head when he fell and that they would make him go to the hospital.

'Well, best get off home,' Joe said, smiling at Tom.

'Joe.' Tom's hand shot out quickly, grabbing Joe's wrist before he could wonder off. Joe stared into the old man's eyes. Joe had never been this close to Tom and he was surprised to notice just how blue Tom's eyes were. Joe could see that they hid a deep sorrow but were also very youthful and had a childlike sparkle to them.

'Joe, if you were to need someone to share any concerns with, no matter how crazy you thought they were, I want you to know that I would listen.' At that the old man let go of Joe's wrist.

'Thanks, Tom, but I'm good at the minute.'

Joe thought he really should get home as he had no idea how long he had been out. Had his adventure lasted minutes, hours? Then a frightening thought came to him. What if he had been away for a whole day or more! Suddenly fearing another telling-off, Joe ran for home as fast as he could.

As he turned the corner beside his parents' restaurant he quickly made up his mind that he would go in via the restaurant itself, rather than go around the back as his parents preferred. Less chance of being shouted at in front of the customers, he decided.

The restaurant was not full and Joe's mum was busy polishing glasses behind the counter. She looked up as Joe came in.

'All right love, you're back nice and early, well done. Dad's just sorting some dinner so we'll eat in about half an hour. OK?'

Without answering Joe went behind the counter and gave his mum a huge hug.

'Steady on, you'll squeeze all the air out,' his mum joked. Joe felt a double dose of relief. Firstly he was relieved to be safely back home after experiencing such a truly bizarre adventure, and secondly he was very relieved not to be getting grounded once again.

****

After dinner Joe decided to stay in his bedroom, alone with his thoughts. As he sat on his blue swivel chair at his desk he closed his eyes. He recalled being out on the rocks and he pictured the impending thunderstorm in his mind. He could remember making a run for it and he could clearly recall losing his footing and falling.

Likewise he could clearly remember waking up outside of Mrs Berryman's cottage, but what had happened in between?

He moved from his chair and lay on the bed, staring at the ceiling. He could picture Henery's smiling face. He could feel the excitement of the chase from the game of coosing. But was it real? Impossible! People can't travel back in time. He must have been knocked unconscious when he fell on the rocks and then dreamt it all. But if that were true, how could he have been knocked out on the rocks but awoken in an alleyway in the heart of the village?

Suddenly a darker thought came to mind.

'Oh no! Damn it!' he said out loud to himself.

Homework. Joe had completely forgotten that he had been set five pieces of homework during the week and he hadn't done any of them.

Well that was all of Sunday taken care of. He would have to spend all day catching up, he thought gloomily. Oh well, at least there were only two days of term left, then the big summer holidays and of course in five days' time, on the 23rd, there would be a massive party as the whole village gets together for old Tom's one hundredth birthday.

Chapter 5 – School

As Joe set off for school on Tuesday morning, he was surprised to feel a bit sad. It was dawning on him that this was his very last day at Mousehole Primary School. Having spent the last seven years doing the same five-minute walk to school, seeing the same teachers and hanging out with the same friends, all of that was about to change.

For the last few months Joe had been longing for the last day. Not that he was really looking forward to 'big school', rather he loved the long summer holidays and the adventures that he, Zack and Billie would have. But now that he had reached the last day his heart felt heavy.

Joe had rather enjoyed school yesterday. During the lunch break he had summoned up his courage and went and knocked on the headmaster's office door. He knew that Mr Pender didn't really like to be disturbed during his break, but Mr Pender as well as being the headmaster also took the boys' sports lessons and taught the Year Six class in Maths, Science and most importantly for Joe, History.

Obviously Joe was not about to tell Mr Pender that he thought he had time travelled back to 1595 as he would definitely have been thrown out of the office and would probably get an after school detention for wasting the headmaster's lunch break. So instead Joe told Mr Pender that he was helping his parents prepare the celebrations for Tom's one hundredth birthday and that his mum had suggested that Joe write a poem about the history of Mousehole to read out. Mr Pender was not surprised as Joe had a real talent for writing anything; exciting stories, presentations about science or poetry. Joe had won the school literary prize for the last three years in a row. Mr Pender was surprised however to hear that Joe would be reading a poem at the celebrations as Joe was painfully shy and Mr Pender had never succeeded in getting Joe to read out his work to the twenty children in the class, let alone to the whole village.

Pleased to see a student making the most of his potential, Mr Pender willingly gave up his lunch break and also allowed Joe to stay behind after school to get the research completed. They worked their way through the school library where they located the information that Joe had already learnt in his lessons; that Mousehole was once known as Porth Enys, that it was possible that Richard, Earl of Cornwall, gave the village the nickname of Mousehole in 1242 when he needed safety for his boats during a storm and thought that the natural safety the cliffs provided looked like the 'hole of a mouse' and that the Spanish Armada landed on the 23rd of July 1595. This is what Joe had really wanted to know more about.

'Sir,' Joe enquired, 'our school books don't go into very much detail about the Armada landing in the village. Can we go online and find out more?'

'Of course we can.'

Joe had sparked Mr Pender's passion for history, which had always been the headmaster's favourite subject to teach.

'But you will have to wait until tomorrow as it is getting late and your parents will want you back for dinnertime I am sure.'

Well that was yesterday and now tomorrow had arrived. Joe almost broke into a run. He wanted to get to school quickly. As it was the last day of term, Mr Pender had said that they could bring in games, DVDs and do whatever they wanted. Joe knew that Zack was bringing in Austin Powers' *Goldmember*. Unlikely they would be allowed to watch that, Joe thought! Besides he knew what he was going to do. He just had to find out about 1595 and also try to discreetly research time travel. After a few days cold reflection, he had decided that he had not been daydreaming nor was he going mad. Joe had time travelled, he was sure of that, and now he wanted to go back to Henery and explore much more.

That last day at primary school flew by for Joe. He had managed to find out that four Spanish galleons had come to the village on the 23rd of July 1595 bringing two hundred soldiers who landed without much fuss and set about burning the village to the ground. He also learnt that Keigwin House was the only building to survive. Then by luck he stumbled across a report written by Don Carlos de Amesquita who was the commander of the attack. In the report he boasted to King Phillip of Spain that as they razed the houses of Mousehole to the ground, the villagers ran to hide in the nearby church at Paul and that the soldiers had shown no hesitation in burning the church as well.

Joe's blood turned cold. Their homes destroyed, the people trapped in the church. Did everybody die? What had happened to Henery, Trevelyan and all those other children that he had only just met?

Chapter 6 – Panic.

Joe tried his best to enjoy his last afternoon at school. His friends wanted him to join in the games and to scoff as much party food as they could, but Joe's mind was already working on a very serious problem. Today was the 21st of July in Joe's world and also back in Henery's world in 1595. What if he could travel back in time once more and warn everybody as to what would happen to them when the Spanish Armada arrive? Maybe he could get them to leave a day early.

He had tried researching time travel, but none of the books or the internet searches gave him the answer.

As he emptied his school tray and locker and put his chair up on the table for the last time, he felt a deep sense of helplessness. Whilst the other children rushed around shouting and laughing, the school bell chimed out the signal for summer freedom. Joe put his rucksack on his back and ambled through the corridors then out into the playground. As he passed through the school gates, Mr Pender was there giving out a few last words of wisdom to each of the Year Six children.

'Remember, children, the world is what you make it, so go out there and be brilliant. Ah, Joseph Pentreath!' he boomed as Joe approached. Joe looked up and snapped out of his trance.

'Well best of luck with your poem, Joe. I am looking forward to it,' the headmaster said, beaming down at Joe.

'Oh yes. Um, thanks, sir and thanks for all your help with the research, I have learnt a lot.'

'You're welcome.' Mr Pender paused, then said:

'Why the long face, Joe? I thought you'd be racing off to dive in the harbour with everyone else.'

'No not today. I have a friend who is in a lot of trouble and I want to help but I am not sure how I can.'

'Some people just have a certain fate Joe and if you are meant to be able to help then the solution will find you. You have been working hard these last few days. Go and have some fun and then get a good night's sleep and things will seem clearer in the morning.' The headmaster gave him a kindly pat on the back.

Joe gave Mr Pender a weak smile. 'Thanks, sir.'

'See you at Tom's party, Joe.'

'Oh... yes... see you then.' And Joe ambled on his way once more.

****

Joe decided that rather than going straight home, he would go back to where it all began. Maybe, just maybe, it could happen again if he was in the right place.

Cutting through the back lanes, within minutes he was standing on the rocky beach near the South Quay. He gazed out at the horizon and tried to remember what he did last Saturday. Did he say something special? Did he stand somewhere special? Maybe he had moved a particular stone as he ran across the beach to dodge the rain. Yes that's right, Joe suddenly recalled, a stone had moved causing him to slip and fall, but how was he to find that same stone on a beach made up entirely of stones? Joe's heart sank.

'Oh this is impossible!' Joe exclaimed out loud, his frustration suddenly getting the better of him. He just had to try and get back to Henery and warn him as to what terror was about to befall the village. He had to figure it out. He rubbed his temples with his fingers as he thought. All this pressure was making his head ache. Head ache. What if that was it? What if it was being knocked out that had enabled him to time travel? After all, firstly he had fallen over on the rocks and ended up in 1595. Then he had run into that wall at the end of the dark alleyway when being chased by Trevelyan and he had ended up in Mrs Berryman's porchway. Was that it? Joe certainly hoped not. He really didn't fancy the prospect of having to knock himself out on purpose. How would he do it? What if it didn't work and he just ended up giving himself concussion. Worse still, what if he ended up killing himself?

Fed up, Joe started to head for home.

When he reached the steps at the end of the beach, which led up into the quayside car park, he noticed, as always, old Tom sat on his bench with Patch fast asleep on his feet. Instead of gazing out to sea however, today Tom was looking directly at Joe.

'All right there, Joe?'

'Hmm, not really,' Joe replied.

'Take a seat lad. Time we had a chat,' the old man said in a kindly voice, gesturing for Joe to sit down on the bench next to him.

'So then, Joe. Tell me, how is Henery? Is he still the coosing champion?'

Chapter 7 – Tom's Story

Joe actually felt his mouth gaping open as he stared at the old man. How could Tom possibly know about Henery? Joe had made sure that he had told nobody about his adventure.

'It's OK, lad, your secret is safe with me. In fact I'm going to tell you a secret that I haven't talked about in these last eighty-seven years.'

Tom cast a furtive look about the harbour side to make sure that nobody was close enough to hear their conversation. Joe moved his mouth trying to speak, but no words would come out.

Tom stared intensely into Joe's eyes. Again Joe could see that childlike twinkle of energy and mischief in Tom's expression.

'Now, Joe, do not speak, do not think up questions, just listen to me. It is very important that you listen to me and then you must do as I say. Will you do that, Joe?'

Joe nodded, already mesmerized as if caught up in a spell cast by the old man.

'Just before my thirteenth birthday I too was playing on my own over there near Merlin Rock. I had gone to the same spot for three days in a row. I didn't know why, I just felt an inner pull, like a voice in my head telling me to go to the rock every day and look out to sea. I didn't know what I was looking for but I could sense danger. To begin with nothing happened, but on the third day when I looked out across the shimmering water, I could make out four large black dots on the horizon. I watched them as they seemed to get bigger. As they grew in size, I could make out what they were. Four massive Spanish Armada galleons. You've seen them too, haven't you, Joe?'

Again Joe slowly nodded his head, remaining mute.

'And you will again. When the boats were big enough to see, I looked behind to check if anyone else could see them. For that moment however there was nobody on the beach nor up on Gurnick Street and when I looked back out to sea, the damnest thing Joe. Those huge galleons had vanished! Well I set off back along the beach, my head full of confusion. Had I been dreaming? Was I going mad?

'My next surprise came as I hopped back over the rocks. There on the beach near the harbour wall was a small fisherman's shack. Strange, I thought to myself. I had never noticed that before. Curious, I went over and gently tried the door latch. The door was unlocked and opened easily, despite it looking really old. It was dark inside as there were no windows, so I left the door open. I could see a small wooden table, two stools and some fishing nets in the corner.'

'As I moved in to explore, the door suddenly slammed shut behind me. I turned in an instance and ran to the door. I don't like being locked in small places, especially dark ones. Anyway I pulled hard on that door but it was stuck fast and would not open. As I struggled with the latch, I heard a boy laughing. I thought that the older boys had played a trick on me.

"Very funny," I shouted. "Let me out!"

'No sooner had I called out than I heard the latch click and the door opened. The sunlight streamed in blinding me for a moment.'

Tom had such an enthralling way of telling stories that Joe sat silently, entranced, soaking up every word.

'I stepped slowly out of the fisherman's shack and onto the beach. There before me, laughing and hopping from rock to rock, was a lad that I had never seen before.'

'Henery!' Joe and Tom said at exactly the same time. They burst out laughing. Joe had never seen Tom laugh, in fact he suspected that this was the first time that Tom had had a really good laugh in ages.

'That's right Joe, Henery. So you know that I was not in the Mousehole that we know today but I was with Henery, in 1595. Well, as I am sure he has done with you, he introduced me to his gang and to the game of coosing. I was really rather good at it and almost beat Henery one time!' Again the old man laughed as he recalled his adventure.

'One time, Tom? How many times did you visit?' Joe enquired.

'Well I remember that I first went on July 18th, I remember feeling frustrated because I didn't get to go on the next day but then I managed to go every day up until the end.'

Suddenly Tom's expression went from youthful excitement to a dark and depressed look. The old man turned away from Joe and he looked out to sea. He let out a deep sigh.

Joe didn't like to see Tom looking sad like this so he quickly asked, 'Tom, I have been trying to find my way back but I can't.'

There was silence for a moment.

'You will not need to search, you just need to relax and Henery will show you the way.'

'Henery?' Joe said quizzically.

'Yes. You see Henery needed us and somehow he has managed to reach out across time to get us to help him.'

'But how? And why?' The excitement was welling up inside Joe, he could barely sit still. He wanted Tom to show him this very minute, how to get back to 1595.

'You have to look for things that are out of place,' the old man simply said.

'What, like moved and untidy?' Joe was confused.

'No. Out of place in time. For me the first thing I saw was the old fisherman's shack. Turns out that that shack was on the South Beach in 1595 but was destroyed by the Armada. The next day I tried too hard to find the shed again and I missed the next sign that Henery had sent for me. The day after however I was just ambling through the streets, head down sulking, when I saw an old ring just lying there on the ground. As soon as I picked it up I was transported back.'

'Hmmm,' Joe murmured, frowning to himself. 'I didn't see anything old when I went back, I just fell over.'

'It will have been Henery, he will have put something there for you to trip over or land on. So be aware as you go around the village for things you have never noticed before.'

'But why does Henery need me?'

'Because I let him down.' Tom's voice was croaky as he spoke and Joe was sure he saw tears in the old man's piercing blue eyes. Joe didn't know what to say so they both sat silently looking out to sea, as seagulls swooped past going about their daily business of scavenging. Patch awoke from his slumber momentarily to give the gulls a look of disgust.

After a few peaceful moments had passed, Tom broke the silence.

'You see in two days' time, on the 23rd of July, bad things are going to happen for Henery, his family and the rest of the coosing gang. I saw it you see, Joe. I was there that day when the soldiers came ashore. They just killed anyone in sight, men, women, even the children. There was such panic.'

'What did you do?' Joe was spellbound once more.

'Ran, Joe, that's what most people did. Some took to the hills to hide in the trees, but I ran with Henery and his family. They made for the church up at Paul. Henery's dad said that they would be safe in the church as nobody is allowed to fight on holy ground and that God would punish the Spanish if they tried. So we ran as fast as we could up Paul Lane with the Spanish soldiers close on our heels. About halfway up the hill I fell and twisted my knee. I couldn't walk another step, Joe. I thought I was done for. The adults had already run past and hadn't noticed. Luckily for me, big Trevelyan was still making his way up behind. He saw me fall and picked me up in one scoop. He tried to run whilst carrying me but there was still too far to go. We noticed a thick hedgerow nearby so Trevelyan put me down and I crawled into the middle of the hedge and covered myself in leaves and branches.

'A short while later I heard the marching of the soldiers' boots. They trooped past me. I kept so still, I didn't even breathe. I sat tight and in no time the soldiers were coming back down the hill. This time they were laughing and singing.'

'When I was sure that they were out of sight, I crawled out from the hedge and limped up the hill towards Paul village. As I got closer I could see smoke billowing up into the sky. I can still recall the terror as I realised what had happened.

'I ignored the stabbing white-hot pain in my knee and I ran for the church. I was too late, Joe. The church was on fire and the flames were already high when I got there. It was so hot, I just couldn't get close but I could hear them Joe and their screams have haunted me every single day since.'

Silence fell once more as Tom and Joe just stared sadly at each other.

'So you see, Joe,' Tom began, 'you have to stop Henery and the villagers seeking sanctuary in the church. You can't stop the Armada coming, they are already on their way, but you can stop that terrible thing from happening.'

Chapter 8 – Teamwork

'Well, well, stopping home on the first day of the holidays, you do surprise me!' Joe's dad said as he came into the kitchen.

'Maybe,' Joe replied.

'If you are, I could really do with your help, what with Tom's party tomorrow and the restaurant already booked up today, I could do with a young man to be in charge of balloon blowing and bunting hanging. Are you up for that?'

After his chat with Tom yesterday, Joe was feeling less anxious about finding the way back to 1595. If Tom was correct then he just needed to keep his eyes open for 'something out of place in time' and Henery would make sure it would be where Joe could find it.

'Yep, OK then,' Joe replied. He cleared away his breakfast things and went to clean his teeth. As he stood in front of the bathroom mirror, he looked into his own eyes and said out loud:

'I'm ready to help you, Henery,' secretly hoping that something out of place would suddenly present itself to him. But no, everything seemed to be the same as always. Maybe he would go and call on Zack and Billie, they could help with the party preparations. That would get the job done quicker.

As he stepped out onto the harbour front he scanned his surroundings. Kayakers, holiday makers, nothing out of the ordinary. He checked the roadside for anything unusual lying there.

'Look out, Joe!'

Joe had been walking with his head down and hadn't seen Zack come whizzing around the corner on his bike. Zack managed to pull a very impressive swerving skid, leaving a long black line of rubber on the road surface.

'I was just coming to call for you,' Zack said once he had regained his composure.

'I was just going to call for you actually,' Joe said.

'So what shall we do on the first day of freedom? Bike ride or surfing?' said Zack, with his usual thirst for adventure.

'Well actually I have a couple of favours I was going to ask you and Billie to help with.'

'Hmmm. What kind of favours? It's not going to be boring is it? I need adventure this holiday!' Zack exclaimed as he pulled a wheelie on his bike.

'Well firstly I have got to get all the balloons and stuff sorted out for Tom's party. Should be a bit of a laugh as Dad has hired in one of those helium machines to blow them up.'

'Cool, OK, and what's the other favour?'

'I'll tell you later but I promise it is definitely an adventure. Come on, let's go and get Billie.'

When the two friends got to Billie's house, his mum told them that Billie was still in bed and that she would make sure that he would 'get his lazy bones out and down to the restaurant straight away!'

In fact Billie had joined his two best friends within ten minutes. Billie was easily the laziest of the three friends. He loved his lie-ins almost as much as he loved cheesecake and it was the thought of cheesecake that had got him out of bed so quickly. Billie knew that Joe's dad always treated the boys to delicious lemon cheesecake and clotted cream whenever they did any jobs for him.

The three amigos were a good team and got all the bunting and balloons ready by lunchtime, although Zack had swallowed more helium than he should have. He made them laugh by talking in a high-pitched voice, pretending to be Mr Pender, their headmaster, telling Billie and Joe off for laughing in class. Now Zack had a sore throat which he told Joe's mum could only be soothed by a large glass of chilled coke.

Whilst they sat eating lemon cheesecake and sipping their drinks, Joe decided that he was going to tell his best friends all about why he had been off on his own so much this last week. Joe had thought this through very carefully and had decided that, if he enlisted their help, then there would be three pairs of eyes around the village looking for Henery's clues.

Just like Joe had been spellbound by Tom's story, so too Zack and Billie were entranced by Joe's adventure. These boys were best friends and the great thing about best friends is that they are always there for you. At no point did either Billie or Zack laugh at Joe or suggest that he was being silly and making things up. They could see that Joe was deadly serious.

'OK, so this thing that is out of place in time could be anything,' Billie said thoughtfully, when Joe had finished. 'And if, like happened to Tom, there is an old shed or doorway of some sort then maybe all three of us could go through together.'

'I guess so,' Joe replied, his mind starting to race again at the thought of this possibility. 'Tom couldn't save the villagers by himself but if I have you guys with me then I think we have a lot better chance.'

'So cool!' Zack chipped in excitedly. 'A real adventure.'

The three friends agreed that if one of them found an old out of place thing, then he would not touch it but would go and get the other two and they would examine it together. They made a plan as to who was going to search which part of the village and then set off on their separate ways.

For the last week, ever since first seeing the galleons on the horizon, Joe had felt a strong pull towards the South Quay area of the village, so this was the area he was now in charge of searching. He started, once more, at Merlin Rock overlooking Spaniard's Point. There were no galleons to be seen today and nothing happened to him as he ambled over the rocks making his way back to Tom's bench. When he got there, Joe was very surprised to find the bench empty. He had never seen the bench without Tom perched upon it. Maybe he is at home preparing himself for his big day tomorrow? Joe thought.

Joe, Zack and Billie had agreed to meet outside of Keigwin House when their searches were complete. When Joe arrived, Zack was already there, leaning against the old side door to the ancient building.

'No joy?' Zack called out as Joe approached. Joe shook his head.

'Maybe Billie has had better luck....' Zack dropped off in mid-sentence. 'But then again!'

Joe turned to see Billie approaching, eating an ice cream.

'Taking it easy then, Billie?' Zack said sarcastically.

'Well it's like old Tom said, the sign will present itself, relax,' Billie replied with a shrug of his shoulders.

Once again Joe's heart began to feel heavy with sadness. He had completely run out of ideas.

The three lads decided to go and get their bikes. They then spent the next hour cycling round and around the village until they felt hungry once more.

'I'm going in for tea,' Zack announced.

'Fair enough. Thanks for your help today guys,' Joe replied.

They agreed that if anything happened to any of them that evening then they would message one another immediately. If nothing occurred then they must find an excuse to get out of the house early the next day. They decided to meet up on the South Quay at eight a.m. as that was the time the Spanish Armada had arrived on the 23rd July 1595.

With plans made they each headed for home.

Chapter 9 – Henery's Signal

Frustratingly nothing came to Joe's attention that evening. After the restaurant had closed, Joe and his mum put up all the balloons and bunting that the three boys had prepared earlier that day. Once in bed Joe just lay there in the halflight, staring at the ceiling.

Had he missed something? He didn't think so. Were Henery, Trevelyan and all the other children now doomed to die in the church once again?

Lost in his thoughts, Joe drifted off into a tortured sleep. He dreamt of being chased by hideous monsters that he could not escape because no matter how fast he tried to run, it felt as though his feet were stuck in thick treacle. Small children beside him called out for him to save them but he was too scared. It was a restless, sweaty night and then…

TAP, TAP, TAP.

Joe sat bolt upright. He could feel that his T-shirt was damp from sweat. Yes he was awake. He looked at his phone. 6.10 a.m.

TAP, TAP, TAP.

Someone was tapping at his bedroom window. Cautiously Joe eased himself out of bed and edged towards the long thick curtains which covered his window. Not sure what he was expecting to see, Joe felt scared and just a little sick.

He went to the left-hand side of his window, took the curtain in his hand and moved it just enough so that he could peep out.

TAP. TAP.

Joe jumped but also laughed to himself. There standing on his windowsill was a magpie, tapping his pointed beak against the glass. The magpie looked at Joe and then tapped its beak on the windowsill. There at the magpie's feet lay a large old-fashioned metal key.

Instantly Joe felt so excited that his hands were shaking. He fumbled with the lock on his window. As he slid the catch the lock made a clicking noise which startled the little bird and it fluttered off.

Trying to be quiet so as not to disturb his parents, Joe eased the bottom part of his sash window gently up enough for him to reach out through. He took a deep breath in a bid to calm his excitement and steady his hand but, as he did so, he suddenly thought.

Hang on, thought Joe. *If I touch the key I will end up in 1595 without Billie and Zack.* He paused. 'But what if I wait to tell them and then come back to find a seagull has flown off with the key? This could be the only chance.'

Joe decided that he had to seize this moment. He slipped his arm out through the opened window and took hold of the key. Carefully lifting it off the windowsill, he safely brought the key into his bedroom and looked down at it.

This is definitely out of place in time, he thought to himself. The key was big and certainly old, yet it also gleamed like new. Then Joe frowned. Why had nothing happened when he picked up the key? He stood contemplating the issue for a moment and then an ingenious thought came to him.

'Yes, of course, that must be it,' he whispered to himself. Joe was sure he had cracked it. He understood what Henery wanted him to do but he would need help. As the plan developed in his mind he slipped on his shorts, fresh T-shirt and trainers, then ever so carefully opened his bedroom door. He peeped through the gap in his parents' bedroom door. He could see that they were still sound asleep but he knew that they wouldn't be for long. They would want to make an early start in order to prepare all the food for Tom's birthday celebration, planned for lunch time this very day.

Silently he crossed the landing then descended the stairs, making sure not to stand on the last step which always creaked. He decided to go out of the back door which had a Yale lock. This meant that he needed no key to lock it behind him as it would lock automatically as he closed it. His parents therefore wouldn't notice an unlocked door or a missing key and this might just buy him enough time to put his plan into action.

First stage of the plan was to collect Zack and Billie without alerting their parents. Zack's house was closest and Joe was outside within one minute of leaving his own house. He had made sure to check around each corner on his way and, so far, nobody had seen him.

As he stood looking up at Zack's bedroom window the magpie came to mind. Joe decided he would throw little pebbles at Zack's window to tap tap him awake. Joe chose his pebbles carefully. Too big or too sharp and he might just break the window and ruin everything!

Joe selected three suitable pebbles. He launched the first one. It was a good shot, striking the glass giving the desired tap. Joe waited. No movement from the curtains. He launched the remaining two pebbles at the same time.

TAP! TAP!

Initially there was no response, but then the curtains opened to reveal Zack's sleepy and confused face staring blankly down at Joe. Joe held up the old key and beckoned to Zack to come with him. Zack sprang into action instantly. Within a moment he was dressed and had fully opened up his window. Zack and his family lived in the apartment above their ice cream parlour and fortunately Zack's bedroom was not actually that far up. In a couple of quick movements Zack had lowered himself from his windowsill and dropped gracefully to the road below. Clearly Zack has done that many times before, Joe thought.

'Wow! Where did you find this?' Zack asked, now holding the large key in the palm of his hand. Joe quickly went through what had just happened.

'Right we must go and get Billie,' Joe concluded and walked off quickly.

'Ha, that should be a laugh!' Zack mocked. 'We struggle to get him out of bed at ten o'clock let alone this early.'

The two boys made the short trip up the road to Billie's house.

'OK,' Zack whispered, 'as Billie's bedroom is around the back of the house, how are we going to wake him up?'

'That's where we need your climbing skills Zack. I'll give you a bunk-up then you will be able to reach the top of the garden wall. I reckon if you can climb along the wall, you will be able to knock on his window.'

'Yeah,' Zack said as he mulled over the plan. 'I think I can.'

Joe cupped his hands together and Zack put one foot into this cradle. As Joe pushed up, Zack sprang like a cat, his hands grasping the top of the wall. He nimbly pulled himself up onto the wall and, with the balancing skills of a tightrope walker, he swiftly crossed to Billie's window. Zack knocked on the window. There was no movement from within. Zack knocked louder. Still nothing. Zack suddenly had a terrible thought. What if he had got the wrong window? What if this was Billie's big sister's room? How would he explain this to Billie's dad if he was caught knocking on his daughter's bedroom window in the early hours? Panic started to set in just as the curtains burst open.

Much to Zack's relief there was Billie's round face staring back at him, looking somewhat dazed and confused.

'Open the window,' Zack implored.

'Oh yeah, right,' Billie said sleepily as he undid the catch and gently slid the window up.

In a hushed voice, Zack explained everything. When he had finished there was a slight pause as Billie looked down at Joe in the side lane beside the house.

'There is no way I'm climbing out there,' he said in a matter of fact tone.

'Go to the front, I'll see you there in a moment.'

By the time Zack had safely gone back across the garden wall, hopped down into the lane where Joe was waiting and strolled around to the front of the house, Billie appeared at his front door, slice of cake in hand.

'There's no time for that!' Zack said exasperatedly.

'There's always time for cake,' Billie retorted.

'We've got to get a move on,' Joe cut in.

'Where are we going?' Zack and Billie said simultaneously, albeit Billie's mouth was stuffed full with cake.

'No time for questions, the Armada will be landing very soon. Just follow me and I promise I will tell you when we get there.'

The three friends set off, Joe in the lead but with Zack and Billie close on his heels. They took the back lanes, so as to avoid going past the front of Joe's house, until they reached the front of Keigwin House.

'What are we doing here?' Zack asked, excitement making his voice sound more high pitched that usual. Joe stared intently at his best friends.

'Well simply touching the key didn't send us back to 1595, therefore I guess that this key must fit in a door somewhere in the village.'

'And what doors are there in the village today that were also here in 1595?' Billie asked, already knowing the answer.

'Of course, only Keigwin House survived the Spanish invasion,' Zack said, now so excited he thought he would burst.

'Exactly,' Joe said, pleased with how quickly his friends caught on. 'And this is also the very spot where Henery and his friends would meet up to start their coosing game. This must have been a happy place for Henery and that's why he has brought us here. This is where he must have most energy.'

'Yeah but which door? What if it's the cellar? How are we going to get into the house in the first place?' Zack asked, sounding rather panicky.

'It won't be. Don't worry,' Joe said calmly. 'The other day Zack, when we met up here, you were leaning against that big door there, which I think leads to the side alley. I bet that made the right connection and that this key will fit that very door.'

Joe had the key in his hand and walked towards the large wooden outer door.

'The lock looks very rusty,' Billie observed. 'I hope it still works.'

They all paused.

Joe took a deep breath.

'Ready?' he asked his companions.

'Ready!' came the excited but ever so slightly frightened reply.

'OK, each of you grab hold of my T-shirt.'

Billie and Zack did as they were told without hesitation.

Joe reached forward, aiming the key for the lock. As he did so he could feel the key getting hot in the palm of his hand and what's more the key started to shine. Joe successfully engaged the key with the lock.

'It fits,' he whispered, turning to look at his friends.

'Turn it!' Zack demanded.

Joe looked back at the door. The rusty old lock was also now gleaming like new. Joe turned the key and the lock made a smooth clunking sound as the door unlocked. As it did so there was a insanely bright flash of white light.

Chapter 10 – Chaos!

'Look out! MOVE! QUICKLY!' came a gruff voice as the boys were roughly manhandled out of the way.

Their senses were suddenly assaulted by noise, smell and physical contact.

The alleyway was not the quiet back lane that the boys had been expecting, rather it was a hive of activity. Burly men were bustling up and down the passageway, shifting heavy looking crates and shouting urgently to one another.

Not wanting to be flattened into the wall again, the three friends scuttled quickly down the alley towards the back yard of Keigwin House.

'This is no place for children. I have made it clear, women and children must go to the church. You will be safe there, now be off with you!' came the instructions from a tall, thickset man with a grey beard. The boys immediately stood to attention at the commanding presence of this distinguished gentleman. His very stature and well-presented appearance demanded compliance. The gentleman's focus was suddenly drawn away from the boys.

'No, not there, Trevaskis, I want the muskets down on the harbour wall and the pistols upstairs here in the house.'

'Yes of course, Squire Keigwin. Sorry, Sir,' the younger man replied and, without a moment's hesitation, picked up the crate that he had just set down and ran back down the side alley.

The boys looked at each other, mouths open. So here they were, standing in front of the legendary Squire Jenkin Keigwin of whom they had only recently read about in their History lessons. Here he was in the flesh, giving them orders.

'Well!' the Squire boomed, turning back to the boys. 'What are you waiting for?'

To his surprise and annoyance, the boys stood their ground. Billie was the first to find his voice.

'Sir, have the Spanish already landed?'

'Landed? No. Four galleons anchored just off Merlin Rock. Just sitting there looking at us. Well they're in for a shock. I knew this day would come. Been building up my reserves. Men lining the harbour walls, snipers placed in the Watch House. I'll be damned if they think they're taking my village! Now do as I say and get to the church, us men have killing to do!'

Squire Keigwin was indeed an impressive man, Joe thought. He could see excitement in the man's eyes, as if he was actually looking forward to the fight like Joe might look forward to a school football match against fierce rivals from Newlyn school.

'Come on let's get going. We must find Henery and the others quickly, before they all lock themselves in Paul Church,' Joe said as he turned from his friends and started to make his way back up the alleyway and into the square at the front of Keigwin House.

'Knowing Henery he would not have followed the adults' orders straight away and he will probably have run down to the quayside to get a good look at the action,' Joe said turning to Zack who had followed him closely.

'Hey, where's Billie?'

The remaining two boys looked about the square but there was no sign of Billie anywhere. Then, ambling up the alleyway from the rear yard of Keigwin House came the third friend, rubbing his right ear and looking a little sorry for himself.

'Tell me you haven't just tried to steal some cake,' Zack said, mockingly.

'No,' Billie replied crossly.

'What's up then?'

'Well we all know what will happen to Squire Keigwin don't we?'

'Yes,' Zack cut in. 'He will die here defending his home and this will be the only building to survive the raid and one day many years from now, someone will put a plaque on the wall in his memory.' Zack looked pleased with himself, showing that for once he had paid attention in class.

'Exactly,' Billie continued, 'so I thought I would suggest to him that maybe standing up to two hundred soldiers wasn't such a good idea and that he should take the villagers and hide out in the trees.'

'So what happened then?' Joe asked.

'He hit me round the ear and said that he would not listen to such cowardly talk and that he would rather die protecting the village he loves than to run and hide. No honour in that, he said.'

'Fair enough,' Zack said simply.

'OK, down to the Quay,' Joe said, and once again set off in the lead.

Quite a crowd had gathered down on the harbour wall by the time the three friends arrived and, sure enough, there at the very front was Henery, Trevelyan and the rest of the coosing gang.

'Look at this!' Henery called out to Joe. The boys pushed their way through the throngs of people until they were part of the gang.

'The Squire's men have fantastic new muskets,' Henery continued. 'And they are brilliant shots. They will put some holes in the Spanish ships. Let's watch them all sink!' he laughed, almost hysterically.

Joe looked along the line of the sea wall and could see men setting up muskets evenly spread all the way to the very end. He then looked out at the Spanish galleons. Four majestic warships lay anchored just off Merlin Rock. Huge sails fluttered in the sea breeze and Joe could clearly make out the Spanish flag proudly displayed on the stern of each vessel. These were indeed the four very same ships that Joe had seen that day when his dad had been out looking for him. Now, close up, the ships were not just impressive but also they were terrifying.

Shouts could be heard travelling across the calm and tranquil sea and, as Joe strained his eyes to see closer, he was sure that the sailors were lowering several smaller boats into the water. Joe knew that in a very short time these boats would be crammed with the soldiers who would come and wreak havoc on the little village.

Joe turned back to Henery. He looked him straight in the eye and said gravely, 'Henery you need to get out of here. Don't wait. Seriously go now.'

'Come now, Joe, you're not scared are you?' Henery replied defiantly.

'Yes actually. This is not going to end well.' But Joe's voice was suddenly drowned out as each of the muskets were fired in unison. There was a brief silence followed by a huge cheer from the villagers. One of the muskets had found its mark and struck one of the soldiers who had been climbing down a rope ladder from the lead galleon into the landing craft, which now bobbed on the sea awaiting its cargo. The soldier's body first convulsed before going limp as he fell head first into the depths of the ocean.

'They won't like that,' Billie said quietly to Zack. He was of course correct. Loud angry shouts immediately flowed from the lead galleon, which was already positioned side-on to the village.

And then it started.

A very loud bang sounded. Smoke billowed from the gunnels of the warship and a high-pitched whistle could be heard just moments before an almighty crash. The small fisherman's shed, which stood on the beach under the quayside, was decimated as a single cannonball struck. Fragments of splintered wood covered the end of the pier, scattering the villagers who had gathered there. A musket shot fired off from within the crowd, immediately followed by the sound of a woman screaming. A large splinter of wood had speared a musket bearer through the neck and his gun had fired by accident as he fell to the floor.

The boys all looked to one another. The smile that Henery always wore had been wiped away and for the first time Joe saw worry on his face. Trevelyan also appeared so worried that he had turned pale and looked as if he was about to be sick.

A second boom and flash came from the Armada. Again came the high-pitched whistle, but this time directly over their heads. Everybody on the pier crouched low to the ground. Another almighty crash, this time making the harbour wall shake. This cannonball had struck at the heart of the village, taking out numerous houses.

Whilst the villagers had been distracted by the volley of cannon fire, the rowing boats filled with soldiers had made good progress and were within one hundred metres of the beach.

'Run!' came the call that signalled chaos. The huge crowd of people all tried to make a break for it at the same time. There simply wasn't enough room on the harbour wall for everyone to move at the same time, so in their panic people pushed and shoved one another as their survival instincts kicked in. One old man lost his footing and fell into the harbour, whilst a woman scooped up her screaming child who had fallen and cut its knees.

'To the church!' Henery called out to his gang as he sped off, the others loyally close behind.

'No!' Joe shouted after them, but it was too late. The crowd closed in around Joe and he quickly lost sight of Henery. Fortunately Joe knew the route Henery would take to get to the church and it was fortunate that Joe was a fast runner. Once off the harbour wall, Joe, Billie and Zack were able to break free from the crowd that had been obstructing their way. Opting for the back lanes and the short cut past the old mill, Joe caught up with Henery by the time his gang had reached the foot of the hill which leads up to the village of Paul, where the church was situated.

'Stop, Henery. Stop!' Joe grabbed Henery's shirt and pulled him to a stop. 'You have to listen to me.'

'There is no time to waste, Joe.'

'I know and we must hide but not in the church,' Joe blurted out, his lungs burning like they were on fire. He had had to run very fast to get level with Henery.

'We must. Squire Keigwin has commanded us to seek refuge there and Father agrees. Nobody is allowed to fight on holy ground, so come on let's make sure the gang are safe.'

Henery made a move to run up the hill but Joe took a firm hold of him just as Zack, Billie and Trevelyan caught them up.

'No,' said Joe in the most authoritative voice that he could muster. Henery shook free of Joe's hold.

'Listen to him!' Zack and Billie demanded at the same time. Joe thought quickly, how could he convince Henery? Then it came to him.

'In my village we have experienced the Armada before. The elders also made sure the people hid in the church, but when the soldiers came they did not regard our church as holy ground and they burnt it down. If you go to the church you will all be burnt to death, it is all part of their evil plan. We must get everyone to hide in the woods instead.'

Henery stood silently, weighing up what Joe had just told him.

'That's why you hadn't heard of my village, it's because the Armada have already destroyed it and that's why I've come here to your village,' Joe fibbed, trying his very best to convince Henery to see sense.

Henery stared intently at Joe and then each to Zack and Billie in turn.

'He's telling the truth,' Zack interjected, 'we saw it too. Joe is right, you must listen to him.'

Other villagers ran past them as they stood staring at each other. A group of women with small children started to make their way up the hill. Henery watched after them.

'Gonn Konvedhav,' murmered Henerey, lapsing into his mother tongue in the heat of the moment. 'In that case we'd better find father, the adults won't listen to us children.'

Running back into the village was no easy task, as they were pushing against the flow of mothers and children all following the orders and making for the sanctuary of the church. Some of the very old men had armed themselves with equipment like scythes and shovels and were taking up defensive positions near to the foot of the hill.

'Have you seen father?' Henery called out to a particularly old weather-beaten man, who was stood leaning on a rake.

'Taking up position at the mill. Hey, but you're not to go down there! Women and children up to the church.'

Before any of the old men could react, Henery and the entire gang side-stepped them and made off at top speed to the mill. As they ran they could hear gunfire in the distance. Joe guessed that by now the Spanish soldiers would have landed and would be making their way up the beach, facing a very limited resistance from the few remaining musket-bearers on the harbour front.

As they reached the mill Joe could see one of the Squire's men giving the local men a very quick lesson in how to use a pistol. Joe's heart felt sad, what hope did they have against trained soldiers!

'Father, father you must come and help me!' Henery called out from a distance. Henery's father looked up from the pistol that he was examining. Joe thought that Henery's father had a very kind face. His soft brown eyes seem to smile at them, despite his obvious worry.

'Henery, you should not be here son. Your mother has already taken your brother and sister up to the church and you must go too.'

'What? Oh no!' Henery exclaimed, 'the Spanish will burn it down!'

'Nonsense, lad. They'd have to get past me first.' Henery's dad smiled and put an arm around his eldest son. Joe could tell that Henery's dad was pretending not to be scared, but that he was as terrified as everyone else that day.

The gunfire suddenly got louder and smoke also rose near to the beach.

'Damn!' another local man swore, 'they're torching the village!'

'That's enough now,' Henery's dad said, letting go of his son. 'Go and look after your mother.' Henery gave his dad one last hug before turning back to face the gang, tears clearly welling up in his eyes.

Against his better judgment Joe announced, 'Henery, we will have to go to the church after all. We must get your family out of there.'

So once again the whole gang were on the run.

Chapter 11 – The Church

'That's it, boys, safely in, the Lord will watch over you now,' smiled the vicar who was stood at the gates to the churchyard, ushering in the last of the old folk who had successfully made the long hike up the hill from the village.

'Reverend, are my family in the church?'

'Yes, Henery, unlike some who have not put their faith in the Lord and have chosen to hide in the woods and take their chances, your family have seen sense and are safely gathered in.'

Upon hearing this, the boys swiftly made their way into the crowded church. To Joe's dismay it was very full. He looked at the worried little faces of the young children, the sad faces of their mothers who held them close and the tired strained faces of the elderly who had struggled to make it up the steep hill on a hot, sunny day.

Once again Henery's coosing skills came to his assistance as he was able to quickly scan the crowd and pick out his family gathered together in the far corner of the church. Henery and Joe wasted no time and skillfully wove through the crowd. The remaining members of the coosing gang also speedily reunited themselves with their families, whilst Zack and Billie went back outside to keep watch.

'There you are, Henery, I couldn't find you anywhere! I have been frantic with worry!' Henery's mum almost sobbed with relief as she squeezed her eldest child close to her.

'Mother, listen, we must get out of here,' Henery pleaded as he wriggled out of her vice-like grip.

'Nonesense Henery. Now calm down, we are safe here. We must pray to the Lord to keep your father safe from harm.'

'Listen to your mother Henery,' an old lady chipped in who sat nearby, 'we don't want any hysterics around the young ones, you'll only start a panic.'

****

Meanwhile the situation outside was getting very serious. Zack had climbed up onto the churchyard wall, much to the protest of the vicar and his churchwarden.

'Get down, lad. Everybody is in now and we are going to lock and barricade the doors, so you need to get inside.'

Gunshots could be heard, getting closer by the minute.

'Just a second more,' Zack called down, straining to peer through the trees to the roadway. Zack could see past the first corner from his elevated position. There was another loud bang followed by an even bigger cheer and then Zack saw them. Almost thirty fully armed Spanish soldiers came marching at speed up the hill, making directly for the church.

'Bloody hell!' Zack exclaimed, sort of falling and jumping off the high wall at the same time. He yelped in pain as he hit the ground.

'Are you OK?' Billie asked as he bent down to help his friend up. The vicar and the churchwarden also scurried over to assist Zack to his feet.

'Oh no!' Zack wailed. 'My ankle, I can't put any weight on it.'

'Come on let's get you inside,' said the vicar in a calm and sympathetic way, as he and the warden took hold either side of him and helped him to hobble into the church.

'They're coming, Billie,' Zack whispered. 'About thirty of them, all with guns.'

'Attend me all!' the vicar called out once they were safely inside. 'The evil is nearly upon us. I need every capable man to help barricade all of the doors.'

'No!' Joe called out as the vicar began to repeat himself in Cornish, but it was too late. Everything Tom had warned him about had now happened but this time Joe, Zack and Billie were also trapped inside the church to face that grim fate that awaited the villagers.

Chapter 12 – Fire!

It did not take long for the villagers to move the large pews and stack them up against the two large church doors. There was no way anyone would be getting in now, but worse still, there was no way anyone would be able to get out either. No sooner had the defences been put in place then voices were heard outside. First came the loud knocking on the main door, then what sounded like commands called out in Spanish, which nobody understood.

'Ignore them,' the vicar said to his congregation, in a hushed tone. 'We will drown out their voices with our prayers.'

The villagers all crouched on their knees and followed the instructions and incantations of their spiritual leader. Meanwhile Joe and Henery moved between the crowds and assembled the coosing gang at the back of the church.

'What now?' Billie asked. Everybody turned to look at Joe.

'The Spanish soldiers outside will be preparing to set fire to this building. Tom did tell me that if the worst happened and we should find ourselves in here then we must look for the escape tunnel,' Joe said thoughtfully.

'The what?' Zack asked curiously.

'The escape tunnel. Most churches had one in these times because they were regularly attacked and robbed. They made secret escape routes so that they could quickly and safely get the religious artefacts out.'

'Well we better be quick!' Zack exclaimed, 'look!'

Everybody's eyes followed to where Zack was pointing. They could all see smoke billowing into the entrance hall under the main door.

'And there!' Trevelyan called, pointing to the small door on the opposite side of the church. It was clear that the soldiers had set a ring of fire all around the church. Surely there could be no escape now?

'The vicar,' Joe said, 'he must know.' Joe hurriedly made his way towards the pulpit where the vicar now led the villagers in prayer. Just as he got to the front there was an almighty crash as a fireball was catapulted through the large glass window above the altar. The villagers screamed and scattered to the side walls as the fireball exploded next to one of the main pillars. In an instance the long ceremonial banner that stretched from the rafters, down the pillar to the floor, caught fire. Bright orange and blue flames licked up the pillar and set fire to the dry wood in the church roof. The younger children and some of the older villagers started to cough as they breathed in the smoke that was starting to fill the main hall.

'Reverend,' Joe began, as the vicar stumbled down from his pulpit. 'Where is the escape tunnel?'

'I never believed men could do something so wicked,' the vicar commented, blankly starring at the cross of Jesus which had fallen off the altar and lay broken on the church floor.

'Reverend, there has to be an escape tunnel, where is it?' Joe shook the vicar by the arms snapping him out of his morbid trance.

'The doorway is down in the basement.'

'Good, how do we get down there?' Henery interjected, now standing shoulder to shoulder with Joe.

'The stairs in the bell tower. But it's no use.'

'Why not?' Both boys said together.

'It's never been used, the door is locked and the key has been lost many years ago,' the vicar replied, suddenly looking without hope.

Joe was very aware that more and more people were suffering from the smoke as the church filled with fumes. Suddenly Billie pushed past Joe and scrambled up the steps of the pulpit.

'Listen, everyone,' Billie called out in a surprisingly strong and confident voice. 'You must all lie down and get your faces as close to the floor as possible, it will keep the smoke from you for a bit longer. Help will come!'

The people listened and all began lowering themselves to reach the cleaner air.

'Come on, Joe, we'll smash the door in. Come on!' Henery commanded before heading off to a small door at the side of the altar. Joe followed, quickly pursued by Billie and Trevelyan who were helping the limping Zack.

The little door creaked as Henery pushed it open. The bell tower was simply a small, empty box-shaped room with four ropes hanging down, each connected to a massive bell which, this morning, had been chiming constantly to warn the villagers of danger and to encourage them to seek the sanctuary of the church. In the far corner there was a trapdoor in the floor. Henery was first to it. The trapdoor had a large metal ring in the middle which Henery used to pull it open with ease. Underneath was revealed a dark hole with granite steps leading down into the unknown.

'It's too dark,' Trevelyan complained. 'We'll get lost.'

'Hang on,' Joe said calmly. He ran back out into the church hall, which by now was half full of smoke. In a moment he returned carrying a burning piece of wood which had been part of a roof beam which had just collapsed. With torch in hand Joe now led the way down the steep damp steps, into the darkness below.

Chapter 13 – Trapped.

There was another small box-shaped room at the bottom of the steps. As Joe's eyes became accustomed to the dim light, he could make out that there was a long, narrow, musty smelling dark corridor leading out from the little basement room. With only the light from the flickering flames to guide their way, the little gang of comrades cautiously made their way forward. Joe obviously in the lead with Henery up close behind him, then came Zack doing his best to keep up and occasionally helped by Billie. Trevelyan brought up the rear.

'Shh. Stop everybody. Quiet. There is a noise ahead,' Joe whispered.

Everybody stopped and held their breath. Joe could just see that a few yards ahead, the tunnel took a bend to the left.

'There did you hear that?'

'Yes,' Henery replied, 'sounds like someone is coming around the corner.'

'Christ!' Zack blurted out. 'Do you think the soldiers know there is a secret entrance and they're coming in from the other end?'

There was another sound, like a stone falling, then a squeak and to the boy's horror three very large fat rats came scuttling around the corner straight at them. Joe and Henery kept silent and swiftly sidestepped the rats but the other three boys were not so quick and the rats' tails brushed their ankles making them swear out loud!

'OK,' Zack said, his voice quivering, 'I've had enough of this pants. Let's get out of here.'

'I'll check around the corner,' Joe said, keeping himself composed despite the terror that he felt inside.

They all edged forward once more. As they rounded the corner Joe could make out the image of a door blocking the passageway.

'We're there,' he whispered.

'Thank the Lord!' Zack exclaimed.

Joe approached the door, his hand outstretched in front of him. As his fingers made contact his heart sank. The door was cold to the touch.

'Damn!'

'What's the matter, Joe?' Billie asked.

'The door. It's not made of wood. It's made of metal. There's no way we'll be able to smash it down.'

'Is it locked?' Henery enquired. Joe felt for the latch. He pulled. Nothing. Henery tried. Big

Trevelyan tried but all failed to budge the heavy blockade.

'The vicar was right, it is locked. We have no key and we cannot break it down.' Joe sighed now, disheartened.

'Brilliant!' Zack said sarcastically. 'So we have the choice of going back and burning to death or staying here and being suffocated underground.'

Joe looked at each of his friends. 'I'm really sorry guys, I should never have got you into this. Now we are all going to die.'

Chapter 14 – Missing.

'Have you seen Joe?'

'What?' Mrs Pentreath said looking up from the birthday cake she was very carefully decorating.

'He's not in his room. Has he been down for breakfast?' her husband enquired.

'No, I thought you'd sent him out on an errand.'

Joe's mum put down the icing bag, having successfully completed the happy birthday message on the top of Tom's cake.

'It's not like him to go without breakfast.'

'Damn, I really need everyone's help today!' Joe's dad blurted out, his face turning red with anger. 'He knows how busy we are when there is a large party to organise, I haven't got time to go hunting the village for him again.'

Mr and Mrs Pentreath were suddenly distracted by a tapping on the restaurant window. It was Mrs Treloar, Zack's mum. Mrs Pentreath went across and unlocked the restaurant door.

'Have you seen Zack? Is he here with Joe?' Mrs Treloar's face showed a pained worry.

'No. No lazy boys here!' Mr Pentreath called out, as he stormed off into the kitchen to continue preparing the food for old Tom's 100th birthday celebration which was due to start at midday, just a few hours away.

'Come in, Alice,' Joe's mum said kindly, showing Mrs Treloar to a seat. Just as she returned to lock the restaurant door she heard a shout from further up Fore Street.

'Wait, Annie, wait!' Joe's mum looked up the street and saw Mrs Trembath, Billie's mum, running down the hill.

'Have you seen Billie?' she panted as she almost hurtled through the restaurant door.

'Err, no. No,' Annie Pentreath managed as she ushered Becky Trembath over to the seat next to Zack's mum.

'Oh dear, oh dear,' Mrs Trembath continued. 'I took my little Billie his favourite breakfast in bed but he was not there, his bed all of a mess, like he'd been snatched in the night!' She started to sob.

'They probably hatched a plan to have an early morning adventure before the party. You know what the three of them are like. Over active imaginations,' Zack's mum said crossly.

'I don't know, Alice,' Joe's mum replied. 'Although Joe often forgets about time once he is out, he normally tells me where he is going and he knows we need help this morning. No I'm not happy with this, something is not right.'

This started Mrs Trembath sobbing.

'I'm going to phone the police,' Mrs Pentreath said decisively, reaching for her mobile.

****

Within the hour the village was a hive of activity. Sergeant Angwin had arrived from Penzance police station, with four officers and a tracker dog.

'We'll have to search each of the lads' rooms and check their computers for any clues as to what they have been planning,' He told all the parents, who had now assembled in the restaurant amongst all the party balloons and streamers.

'I've told the inspector and he's on his way. If anyone can find them Inspector Hudson can, so no need for worry. He's already asked for the helicopter and that's on its way from police headquarters,' the Sergeant continued, hoping to calm Billie's mum who by now was hysterical. Even Joe's dad was concerned now and was also thinking that something bad must have happened to the boys.

The party preparations were put on hold whilst Joe's parents served up coffee and cake to all those gathered, and they waited for the police officers to complete their searches. As he poured more coffee, Joe's dad noticed a police Land Rover pull up on the harbour front. Sergeant Angwin and the police dog-handler walked over and greeted the tall, thin, smartly dressed officer who got out of the passenger's side. Joe's dad could see that they were involved in an intense conversation, which resulted in the tall man pointing out directions to the others. Mr Pentreath then saw Sergeant Angwin point at the restaurant and immediately the tall police officer took long strides in their direction.

'Good morning, everyone, I am Inspector Hudson.' The tall man announced as he entered the restaurant. 'Could I have a private moment with Mr and Mrs Pentreath, please?'

Joe's parents suddenly felt sick with worry. Had the police found out something? Was Joe hurt, or worse?

'Come through,' Joe's dad said, showing the inspector through into their kitchen.

'Have you found something?' Joe's mum said, doing her best now to hold back her tears.

'Well,' The inspector began, 'we have found some Facebook conversations which suggest that the three boys were all planning something together, something they did not want anyone else to find out about and it seems that your Joe was encouraging young Zack and Billie to help him with this plan.'

Mr and Mrs Pentreath sat stunned and silent. Of course they had no idea what had been on Joe's mind recently as Joe had been very careful with his secret.

'Has Joe been acting oddly at all recently?' the inspector enquired.

'How do you mean?' Joe's mum asked.

'Well, has he been quieter than usual, or spending more time on his own?'

Joe's parents looked at each other in silence for a moment.

'Well he has been late home a few times recently and you have had to go and look for him, haven't you love?' Mrs Pentreath said, breaking the silence.

'Yes that's true, he seems to be daydreaming more than ever at the moment,' Joe's dad added.

'OK,' the inspector said, making a note in his pocket book. 'And where have you found him on those occasions?'

'Down on the South Quay, talking to old Tom most of the time,' Mr Pentreath answered.

'Old Tom?' Inspector Hudson asked simply.

'Yes, Tom Tregenza,' Joe's mum replied. 'We were all preparing for Tom's one hundredth birthday celebrations today.'

'And where does Mr Tregenza live?'

Joe's parents described to the Inspector how to find Tom's little fisherman's cottage. Inspector Hudson explained that he would send officers to search the South Quay and beach towards Spaniard's Point and that he and Sergeant Angwin would go and see if old Tom could help with finding the boys.

While the officers carried out their duties, Joe's parents returned to the restaurant and discussed the situation with Zack and Billie's parents. By the time they had talked through the various possible predicaments the boys may have got themselves into, the inspector had returned, a troubled look upon his face.

'What is it? What did Tom tell you?' Joe's dad asked impatiently.

'Nothing,' The inspector replied.

'Nothing!' The group of parents exclaimed in unison.

'It would appear that Tom Tregenza is also missing.'

Chapter 15 – The End.

The boys stood in silence in the cold, damp tunnel, just the flames from the fire torch in Joe's hand making a crackling noise.

'Well there's no point in staying down here,' Henery said, breaking the tension between them.

'Well I don't fancy going up there and becoming toast!' Zack retorted with more sarcasm.

'Shh!' Joe sounded.

'I'm not going to shh,' Zack replied, frowning at Joe.

'Seriously, Zack, shut up and listen,' Joe said sternly.

As the group stood motionless they could hear it, a sort of metal scrapping on metal noise.

'It's coming from the door,' Billie whispered.

There was a clink then a clunk.

'Oh my God, what if the Spaniards have found the secret tunnel and have made it in from the other end!' Trevelyan said.

This seemed the most likely answer all of the boys realised as they started to back away from the door. A slow creaking noise now emanated from the rusty hinges and the door began to open before their very eyes.

'Joe! Joe!' came a voice through the widening gap.

The voice sounded familiar to Joe and it certainly wasn't a Spanish accent.

'Tom? Tom, is that you?' Joe stepped forward reaching for the door with one hand and moving the torch closer to shed light on the figure that was approaching out of the shadows with the other. As he pulled the door fully open, there was old Tom waiting with a big smile on his face.

'Everybody OK?' The old man asked.

'Er, um yes, well Zack's hurt his ankle, but, but how did you get here and how did you open the door?' Joe stammered.

'There's no time for all that now,' Tom said firmly, 'we must get out of here, there is still work to do. Follow me!' Considering just how old Tom was, he moved surprisingly quickly. He had his own modern-day torch with him which lit up the tunnel so well that Joe did not need the fire torch anymore, so he blew it out with a huge puff.

After just a few twists and turns the boys saw that daylight was streaming into the tunnel just ahead of them.

'Nearly there now,' Tom called back down the line. Although Tom moved swiftly for an old man, he progressed slow enough for Zack to keep up. Gradually the boys' eyes began to adjust to the influx of light and they could see a set of stone steps leading out of the tunnel.

'Right, keep quiet when we get up the steps,' Tom said as he slowly climbed the stone staircase. The group followed him closely and to the boys' surprise they found that the steps led up into a haybarn.

To their great relief all five boys were now safely out of the tunnel and stood in a semicircle looking in wonder at old Tom, who carefully closed the lid on the trapdoor which they had just climbed through. As Tom turned to face them they saw that he focused his gaze on Henery.

'We've solved it this time, Henery, now you will be able to rest in peace,' the old man said in a hushed voice.

Joe looked to Henery and could see that he had tears in his eyes and one big drop escaped and ran down his cheek as he let out a big smile. To everyone's surprise the lad rushed forward and gave Tom a big hug.

'Thank you, Tom. I knew you hadn't forgotten me.'

Joe could also see that Tom had tears of joy in his eyes. Maybe the nightmare that Tom had carried with him all his very long life would now be lifted.

'Sorry but where are we?' Billie asked, interrupting the moment.

'Just a field away from the church,' Tom replied.

'So how on earth did you find us Tom?' Joe enquired.

'Well you boys have caused quite a panic back home, setting off so early in the morning like that. You've got your parents so worried that they've called the police. There's even a helicopter out looking for you.'

Joe, Zack and Billie looked sheepishly at one another. They never meant to cause any upset to their parents.

'With you chaps having been gone for so long I realised that there must be a problem and I feared that you had gone to the church after all,' Tom continued.

The five boys stood motionless as they listened to the old man. Tom told them that he had decided to make for the church in the hope that Henery had also left a sign for him so that he too could come and help.

'As I approached the church,' Tom explained, 'the church bells started to ring. It made me jump and I let go of Patch's lead. Quick as a flash old Patch was off. I called after him but he paid me no attention. He had squeezed under the gate to a field we had just passed and ran at great speed through the long grass, barking all the while. It took me a few moments to untie the gate and start my way after him, by which time he was out of sight. I called out. No answer. I kept shouting as I cut my way through the tall grass and when I got near the middle of the field I could hear a low deep growl and a scrabbling noise. I made my way towards the noise, worried that he'd got himself stuck down a badger hole or worse stepped on a fox trap.'

The old man looked each boy in the eye then continued:

'When I caught up with Patch, I found him digging frantically in the earth. I peered down to see what he was after and there under the thick grass, half buried in the ground was an old iron ring. 'Twas like a door knocker that people used to have on their front doors years back. As I bent down to look closer, I noticed that there was a thick rope attached to it and the rope led out into the grass. I pulled the grass roots away enough so that I could take hold of the rope. No sooner had I put my hands around that rope then there was a flash of light, the like of which was familiar to me and I was instantly transported here, holding the rope to the lid of that trapdoor. Poor old Patch was nowhere to be seen but I knew that my loyal friend had played his part and I was ready to do the rest. I pulled on that rope and lifted the trapdoor and to my further surprise there I saw a large key attached to the underside of the lid, a key that to my great relief was the key to the door down in the tunnel.'

Tom paused whilst the boys took in what he had told them.

There was no time for contemplation however. The little group suddenly had their attention disrupted as they heard a shot fired, quickly followed by a woman's scream.

'The Spanish soldiers are still close by and there is more work for us to do. Time is of the essence, we must act quickly,' the old man said, seriousness returning to his face.

'Yes.' Joe agreed, 'we can't leave the villagers in the church to die. We must show them the secret entrance.'

Joe made a move towards the tunnel entrance.

'Wait!' Tom exclaimed, catching hold of Joe quickly by the forearm.

'Everyone is very upset and worried about you boys back home. You must go home now and show them that you are safe.'

'But we can't leave, we have to show the villagers the way out, we can't leave them to burn!' Joe's face had turned red with anger as he frowned at Tom.

'Listen, Joe, Henery is safe and that is your mission completed, you have saved him. You did more than I could ever do on my own. Now you must go home. Henery, Trevelyan and I will save the others,' Tom replied calmly.

'But Tom you must come back with us!' Joe, Zack and Billie all said in unison. Joe continued, 'As you said, the village is waiting.'

'Yes,' Tom said firmly. 'This village is waiting for me, here and now. Boys, I'm not coming back. Patch will be waiting back in the field where I left him. He will be upset and confused. I need you boys to go and take care of him for me.'

'But, Tom!' Joe interjected, tears now welling up in his eyes and a lump forming in his throat.

'No Joe. I'm one hundred years old and this is the adventure I've been waiting to finish all my life. Please say sorry to everyone at home and thank them for thinking about me.' Tom started to follow Henery and Trevelyan who were already descending the steps back down into the tunnel.

'Tom, we must help!' Joe implored. Tom stopped and looked back at the three boys for a moment. He knew they were upset.

'You boys really are determined aren't you?' The old man's expression changed. Joe had not seen this look before and sensed a slyness in the old man's words. 'OK, we will need help actually. I will follow Henery and Trevelyan back to the church and ensure that we guide the villagers safely out, but you boys must stay here and close the lid on the trap door. The Spaniards must never find this secret passage. Wait here until we return, I will give the door four knocks so that you know it is us.'

The boys all nodded in agreement.

'Once I have gone down the steps,' Tom continued, 'you must close the door immediately then find a safe place to hide nearby. You must be careful, the lid is very heavy and it will need all three of you to take a firm grasp of the rope at the same time.'

The three friends seemed content with this task.

'Be careful, Tom,' Joe said as Tom disappeared into the darkness of the escape tunnel. Tom simply looked back and gave him a wry smile, leaving Joe with the distinct feeling that he might not see his old friend again.

'Come on then,' Zack said as the remaining three members of the rescue committee gathered around the trapdoor. 'You heard him, let's all take hold together.'

The length of rope that was attached to the heavy iron door lay stretched out along the straw which covered the barn floor. The boys all bent down at the same time and reached for the rope. No sooner had they touched the coarse rope then they were instantly transported away from the barn, away from the dangers of 1595 and back to the field with the thick long grass that Tom had told them about.

Patch yelped in surprise as the boys appeared before him out of thin air.

'Bother it!' Joe exclaimed, 'Tom's tricked us.'

'But how?' Zack asked, bemused, as he bent down and patted Patch.

'The rope, he must have swapped the old rope on the trapdoor with a new one he had brought with him. Now it's brought us home,' Joe explained.

'It's Patch's lead isn't it?' Billie stated.

'Of course,' Zack agreed, 'Tom just uses one of his fishing ropes when he wants to put Patch on a lead and he must have swapped it over before he entered the tunnel to come and find us.'

'I knew he was up to something,' Joe said rather disappointedly.

'Do you think he will be all right?' Billie asked. 'Do you think we really did manage to save them?'

'I don't know,' Joe replied thoughtfully. 'I just don't know.'

'What shall we do with Patch?' Zack interjected. The boys all looked down at the old collie dog who was lying on his stomach whimpering.

'I think he knows that Tom is not coming back.'

Joe bent down and untied the new piece of rope from the old rusty iron ring that was once more half buried in the ground. He slipped the rope around Patch's collar and said, 'Come on then old friend, we'll look after you.' Patch stood up, gave Joe's face a big slobbery lick and gave a little bark, as if to say, 'OK then.'

The three friends decided that it would be best to take Patch to Tom's cottage first of all until they had a chance to talk with their parents. They left the grassy field and set off down Paul Lane back towards the heart of Mousehole village. They agreed that once down in the village they would take the back lanes to get to Tom's cottage as they weren't quite ready to face their parents and they were even less prepared to explain to the police about their adventures.

Fortunately the villagers were preoccupied searching the shoreline for the missing boys and this left the back lanes empty for the little group of adventurers to pass unseen. They had just turned the last corner on the approach to Tom's house when a loud voice sounded behind them.

'Sarge, Sarge they're over here!'

This startled the boys and they turned around quickly to see a young-looking policeman rushing towards them, the older Sergeant hurrying to catch up.

'Wait there, lads!' the younger officer called out. He need not have worried, as the boys were frozen to the spot at the shock of seeing two policemen homing in on them.

'Well now, boys,' Sergeant Angwin began once he had got his breath back, 'you have certainly led us a merry dance. What have you been up to, then?'

The three friends were dumbstruck and looked blankly at one another for a moment. There was no way that they could tell anyone about their adventures, no adult would ever believe them.

'We went to see Tom,' Zack said, cutting the silence.

'Yes,' continued Billie, 'we wanted to be the first to wish him a happy birthday, so we set out early this morning.'

'But when we got to his house, Tom was missing,' Zack cut in again, quite enjoying the chance to tell a fib to a policeman, 'so we have been out looking for him ever since.'

'Hmmm…' Sergeant Angwin murmured, clearly not buying this story. 'And have you found Mr Tregenza?'

'Yes,' Joe answered absent-mindedly.

'And no,' Zack quickly added.

'Yes and no,' the young police constable said. 'Which is it?'

Once again Zack took control of their made-up version of events, 'Well we saw him from a distance but when we got there he had vanished. Just old Patch was there wondering around by himself.'

'So where exactly did you find Patch and where was Mr Tregenza when you last saw him?' the sergeant asked.

'Near to Paul church,' Joe replied, which was true, he just didn't add that they last saw Tom near to Paul church but over four hundred years ago!

'Good, there we are, not too hard to tell the truth was it?' Sergeant Angwin said, smiling at the boys. 'Now I'll go and tell the inspector and we'll soon have this wrapped up in time for lunch,' he added confidently and began to stride off in the direction of the restaurant.

'It's no use,' Joe called after him. 'You won't find him.'

'You leave it to the professionals now boys, we'll find old Tom. Come on everyone to the restaurant, there are some very worried parents that need to see you.'

Within a few minutes the scene at Mr and Mrs Pentreath's restaurant was very emotional. All the mums held each of their sons in a vice-like bear hug grip, tears rolling down their faces and dripping onto the heads of the boys, who looked very embarrassed at all the fuss. Initially their dads looked a bit cross because of all the upset and hassle they had been put through, but when Sergeant Angwin explained that the boys had actually been concerned for Tom and that the three friends had been on a lost person expedition of their own, then they were all suddenly forgiven and actually their fathers looked quite proud. Patch stood outside, with his nose pressed against the restaurant window. He let out a sad little whine as he was clearly missing Tom and wanted him back, too.

Whilst the reunion was taking place Inspector Hudson took Sergeant Angwin to one side in order to get from him the information that the boys had provided about Tom's disappearance.

'Sorry to interrupt,' Inspector Hudson said, joining the group of local people. 'I'm going to need the boys' help. Lads, I need you to come and show our dog-handler exactly where you last saw Tom.'

With that, tears started to well up in Joe's eyes.

'What's the matter?' his mum asked, looking most concerned. Joe turned to face his parents.

'We saw Tom in the fields near to Paul Church, but there is too much time between us now, I don't think we'll be able to find him again,' Joe said solemnly.

'Nonsense, our police dogs are superb at tracking people, you just need to point us in the right direction. No time to waste, let's get to it.' Inspector Hudson didn't wait for a response. He gathered the boys and his officers outside of the restaurant then marched them up Fore Street towards Paul Lane.

For the second time that day Joe, Zack and Billie led a rescue team up the hill to Paul Church. The three friends walked in front with Inspector Hudson and the police dog-handler close behind. Patch had now taken to faithfully following close to Joe's heel. He wasn't very pleased to have Rogan, the police dog, nearby and gave him a low growl anytime he got too close.

When they were just over halfway up the hill, Zack whispered to his friends, 'This is a total waste of time!'

'I know but what else can we do? We can hardly say that we have been time travelling and we left Tom back in 1595 can we?' Joe replied.

Billie and Zack looked blankly back at Joe. None of the boys knew what to do for the best.

Suddenly old Patch let out a loud bark and took off up the hill. Rogan sensed excitement and gave chase pulling his police handler over. The police officer swore as he fell to the ground and Rogan's lead was ripped out of his hands. The two dogs sped off at a furious pace.

'Looks like we won't have to explain after all,' Billie said, 'Look!' He pointed up the hill.

Joe rubbed his eyes in disbelief. There, ambling down the hill towards them as if he had all the time in the world, was Tom.

'Tom!' the boys called out, as they ran past the police officers. Tom looked up and gave them that familiar wry smile.

Patch got to him first, bouncing up and down like a young puppy. The police dog circled them both, barking frantically.

'Good boy, Patch. Good boy,' Tom said bending down to talk softly to his faithful companion.

As the boys approached the old man they all started talking at once.

'We thought you would get caught in the fire.'

'Or the soldiers would catch you.'

'We thought you were going to stay with Henery forever.'

'Are they all OK?'

'What happened?'

'Wait, wait, one at a time,' the old man said laughing.

By this point Inspector Hudson, his officers, Mr and Mrs Pentreath and many of the locals had caught up and gathered around, all pleased to see Tom looking in fine health.

Tom leant forward and whispered to the boys, 'The coosing gang are all safe and Henery is at peace at last, thanks to you.'

The old man then straightened up as best he could and spoke to the gathered crowd.

'I am very sorry for all the fuss I have caused. The 23rd of July is a very special day for me and I had to visit some very old friends and share some of it with them. But I simply couldn't miss out on a party with all my young friends, I hope I'm not too late.'

And with that they made their way back to the restaurant where the whole village had now gathered. The street outside had been closed off and tables and chairs put on the road so that everyone, including the police officers and Rogan could join in the celebration, much to Patch's disapproval.

Joe, Zack and Billie sat at the head of the main table with Tom and as they tucked into all the lovely food that Joe's dad had prepared. Joe leant over to Tom and said, 'I think that this must be the best 23rd of July that the village has ever seen.'

The old man rested back in his seat and looked at everyone who had gathered to wish him a happy birthday.

'Yes, Joe,' he said. 'I think you are probably right.'

Time Traveller's Quiz – Out Of Place In Time.

We hope that you enjoyed Joe's adventure but did you notice that all was not quite as it should be in some of the illustrations?

Tom explained to Joe that in order to time travel he had to look for items that were out of place in time. Apart from the old key which the magpie dropped on Joe's window sill, there were ten other items that were 'out of place in time'.

Now look back through all of the wonderful illustrations and see if you can find them. To see if you have correctly identified all of the objects go online and visit www.haveyouseenjoe.co.uk

Good luck!

R.T.J. Hockin & Joe Mason